Rena's Silver Lining

Rena's Silver Lining

Sandy Knauer Morgan

ISBN-13: 978-0692434802
ISBN-10: 0692434801

Cover art: Sandy Knauer Morgan

Acknowledgments

Thanks, more than I can say, and from the bottom of my heart, to:

Briana Morgan for reading aloud to me and for believing in me.

Cindy Parker for being the first person to make me believe this story was worth sharing.

Teresa Fancher for the many hours dedicated to the final edit.

Chapter 1

(Rena)

The snooze button renders a limited number of reprieves before it finally says *screw you, it's my turn to go back to sleep*. It was a screw me morning; the clock and I snoozed peaceably together for an extra couple of hours. When my eyes finally opened without an intruding alarm, light poured between the blind slats.

I threw back the red satin comforter, a gift delivered to my door two days after my mother's first visit to my new apartment, because the *disgraceful excuse for a bedcovering* (her words) I was using could be viewed as a poor reflection on her. Unfortunately, she neglected to replace the sheets, too, so on this day, the gorgeous red comforter still lived atop a yellow flannel fitted sheet and the orange and green striped top sheet that was the only thing I had to show for my last relationship.

In my rush to get to the shower, as though a couple of seconds would matter when I was already fire-me-please late for work, I failed to notice that the top sheet had wrapped itself around my leg tight enough to require surgical removal. The silver lining was that it hung on for dear life and minimized the carpet burns on my knees when I landed on the floor and skidded across the room. But it did little to protect the heels of my hands.

While standing under the shower, cursing the sting of carpet-burned hands, I pondered a couple other mind-shattering questions: Should I start sleeping on the floor to avoid injury and is it better to be screwed by an inanimate object than to not be screwed at all?

I sliced a sizeable chunk of skin off my bruised but not terribly burned knee with the dull razor I used to scrape the fuzz off my legs, and talked myself out of calling in sick before the third question came to mind. Was my alarm clock more useful than the men I had dated? It was there every day and had willingly screwed me three out of five days a week for the last year. Much as it hurt to admit it, this might have meant Mother was justified in criticizing the men I had dated. But, that didn't mean she still needed to nag me about finding a (her word) *keeper* every time she saw me.

Without doubt, the clock won, hands down. Or hands up as the case would have been if the clock hadn't been digital. It was nine fifty-five, an hour and fifty-five minutes after I should have opened my customer service window at Greenville Water Company's main business office – the last place I ever expected to work. I overslept on the day delinquent customers were scheduled for shut-off and that was inexcusable. Because I failed to wake on time to collect last minute overdue payments, some unfortunate souls might have to go to work without coffee or a shower.

Remembering my experience at Russell Jenky's deli the week before, I hoped it wasn't anyone who worked with the public. My first thought that day was that the new kid must have kicked a slice of dropped meat under the counter to rot again. He was surely another Jenky relative. Otherwise there was no sensible reason I could imagine to keep him and his sloppy work ethic around.

Clarice disagreed about the potential cause of the stink. She believed it had to be one of those exotic cheeses Russell brought in so he could add a gourmet column on the blackboard menu and raise prices. "Whatever it is," she said, "it's rank and has no business in a place where people are fixing to eat."

The smell ended up coming from Russell's wife, Gladys, who worked the register alone during that extremely busy lunch hour, wearing a multi-colored synthetic sweater. When she reached across the counter to deliver the change from my ten, I felt my stomach try to claw its way out through my throat. I held my breath and thanked her, and didn't inhale again until Clarice had finished paying for her meal and we walked away.

"It makes sense if you really think about it," I told Clarice, when my gagging subsided and we settled into the booth farthest away from the cashier. "Shouldn't a sweater make you sweat?"

With much less discussion than we normally devoted to our world-changing hypotheses, we decided *warmer* would be a more appropriate title for that article of clothing, at least for those of us who don't wear them for the purpose of sweating.

I would have to remember to ask Clarice to help me decide if clocks are inanimate. I finished my shower, band-aided a square of toilet paper over my knee to catch the blood, towel-dried my hair, and dressed in gray slacks, a lavender warmer, and my navy slip-on shoes. At least that's what I thought. Clarice informed me later that I was wearing one navy shoe but its odd mate was black.

"Rena," she whined, "you need to get to bed earlier so you can clock in before lunch and wear clothes that match. Maybe you could even put on some of that make-up you cleaned your bank account out to buy. No offense, but you won't ever get moved up looking like this."

By that time I enjoyed Clarice's whine as much as I cherished the advice she was becoming less and less reluctant to offer. But the first time I heard her speak, I thought fate had cursed her with the worst luck possible.

Ann Lyons hauled me into the customer service department on my first day and caught Clarice by surprise as she leaned over to put her purse in a file cabinet drawer. Without giving Clarice a minute to orient herself after rising, Ann asked her to show me around Greenville Water Company. Clarice smiled, sniffed, and said she was glad to meet me. I envied her composure, thinking it must have been positively humiliating to meet the new employee when her head was full of snot.

Ann left us alone and I discretely whispered that it wouldn't offend me if Clarice wanted to blow her nose. I'd wait.

"Girlfriend, I don't need a tissue. This is my regular voice," she explained. "I reckon I needed some offensive trait to counteract this beauty and stave off the heap of men bound to collect at my feet otherwise." She tried to laugh but it came out sounding more like a snort, probably, I thought, another symptom of the condition that caused her to talk like her head was full.

I laughed and said I was sorry, immediately afraid I had made my second big blunder. Surely, she *was* kidding. Clarice was anything but a stud magnet. In fact, she reminded me of Belinda Peakins, a girl I knew in college. Often, the less attractive girls (who would have been my crowd, had I joined one) would drag Belinda along when they went to clubs or parties, so they could ease their disappointment later by realizing someone got less attention from the guys than they did. Belinda, on the other end, laughed about ignoring the jerks that kept hitting on them because she knew she could do better.

After knowing Clarice for less than five minutes, I hoped no one had treated her the way my friends had treated Belinda. I wasn't sure how I felt about her laughing off what she probably perceived as me treating her the same.

I posted a quick reminder in my sub-conscience to look *stave* up in the dictionary, and concentrated the rest of my energy on Clarice's face. I hoped her expression would tell me whether or not she understood that I was laughing with her, and not at her.

Clarice drew the corners of her mouth back a tad bit further, exposing one more oversized, protruding tooth on each side. I wanted to count, because I was sure she must have twice the number of teeth the rest of us grow, but I was already bordering on rude so I focused on her eyes. I thought I saw a glint but couldn't be sure it represented warmth. It might have been a reflection off the rhinestone studs in the black plastic frames of her glasses.

"Let's just throw this out on the table straight away," she said. She tried another smile that was so wide she had to slurp to keep saliva from dripping out the corners of her mouth. She stretched her lips over her teeth and swallowed.

"Girlfriend, I own mirrors and I've been hearing my voice my whole life. You don't need to pretend you're blind or that I'm anything other than what I am. I don't. I like me just fine the way I am." She paused to slurp again before she said she hoped I would too.

I said thanks because I couldn't think of anything better to say.

"One more thing," she added. "I try to avoid the paparazzi, so if you're somebody famous we'll have to restrict our meetings to private places."

I wasn't sure I wanted her to call me girlfriend, but was pretty sure I liked Clarice just the way she was otherwise.

My life changed that day. Clarice McDaniels exorcised the normal, boring, twenty-four-year-old, semi-depressed, and slightly neurotic, Rena Boiles right in the middle of trying to convince the world that I was smarter, more beautiful, saner, and more successful than I truly was, or than my mother pretended I was when we weren't alone. Clarice McDaniels shamed the all-American-version of the liberated-woman right out of me, and truly liberated me from the box that controlled my life. Instantly.

Before meeting Clarice, I had never considered the important things in life, like the hidden meaning in my alarm clock, or the inappropriate titling of clothing. And nobody called me girlfriend.

Clarice turned the lights on and introduced me to a world I had never seen before. Seeing the world through Clarice's glow is about as good as it gets.

Chapter 2

After a long day of concentrated effort, I knew I had rearranged and reworded everything I possibly could. My resume already portrayed me more favorably than it should have, considering my limited work experience, but I still wasn't satisfied. When my brain ached and still no further fabricating came forward, I saved the changes and hit the print command.

To the envy of my roommate, the regret of my advisors, and the absolute disgust of most of my peers, I had completed three years of college before working my first job. Knowing how I ranked schoolwork somewhere between shining the neighbors' hubcaps and eating dirt, Dad covered all of my expenses while I was in school. He promised he wouldn't mention money or my partying as long as I delivered passing grades with the bills. And I had to live in the dorm. We each lived up to our side of that deal – sort of.

At the end of the third year, my academic advisor suggested I work during the summer break so I would have something to put on my resume when I graduated. The idea of surrendering pool time for a paragraph on a resume didn't exactly generate a wave of excitement but I agreed to consider her suggestion.

Finding an easy way out was one of my stronger talents, so I worked as a lifeguard at the country club that summer, spending most of my time on the side of the pool with friends. The most difficult responsibilities of the job were testing the chlorine level of the water twice a shift, and sending the Anderson children back to the shallow end of the pool when they occasionally floated too far in the wrong direction.

With degree in hand the next summer I went to work as a receptionist for Jim Crane, an obstetrician who also happened to be my grandfather's oldest friend. I matured during that year enough to realize I didn't want to stay in a receptionist position forever.

Each day, I finished my work as quickly as possible and then sat with the appointment scheduler, secretary, or bookkeeper, learning everything I could about their positions. I kept that up for a year, never missing a day and putting in as many overtime hours as the manager allowed. My goal was to replace the manager when she retired.

Dr. Crane ruined that plan by retiring before she did and there was no way I could replace him. He called us into the conference room mid-May to announce that he would retire at the end of the summer. He offered references, time off for interviews, and his blessings to those of us who wanted to go ahead and look for new jobs.

As the other employees filed out of the conference room, he asked me to remain and close the door.

"Rena, I hired you originally because your grandfather is a friend of mine and I wanted to help out." It sounded like one of those beginnings that could only get worse, so I wasn't sure I wanted to hear any more. I offered a little smile and reminded him that I should be at my desk in case the phone rang.

"It's okay, the other girls will get it," he said, erasing any hope that I might avoid the conversation.

"You surprised this old man. I appreciate the work you've done, and have taken a great deal of pleasure in watching your development. I want you to go out there now and look for a more challenging position – something at least at an assistant manager level. You have the degree, and you're certainly capable. Don't wait for me to leave,

7

because then you'll have another group to compete with. Start looking now."

With Dr. Crane's motivational speech in mind, I grabbed the resume off of the printer, scanned it for mistakes, and headed out to answer the water company's ad for an assistant manager of the Human Resources Department.

The interview went well, I thought. Ann Lyons actually seemed impressed with my skimpy resume, and she was overjoyed with the reference letter Dr. Crane had given me. I was positive she was going to offer me the position but, at the conclusion of the interview, she offered me a customer service representative job instead.

She must have seen my disappointment because she came back with what I would later realize was a patronizing spiel. "All employees of Greenville Water Service start at the bottom and work their way up," she explained. "The current CEO of GWS started out waxing floors in the old building while he was still in high school. And look where he ended up."

Her head-bobbing was contagious. Before she finished, I was nodding with her and able to smile. By the time I walked out of her office with my employee manual and parking pass in hand, Ann Lyons had convinced me that she had offered me the chance of a lifetime. I would start at the bottom and work my way up, experiencing every aspect of the organization. In no time, I would advance into the position that I had come there seeking, with a thorough understanding of the work my employees would do.

Clarice didn't laugh at me for swallowing Ann's bait. Clarice never laughed at anyone except herself, nor did she say I told you so (a single one of the many times I deserved it). Instead, she threw her head back like she was looking to heaven for help, rolled her face from side to side, and said, "Mercy, Girlfriend, you have a college degree and she pulled that on you?"

Before the flicker of shame I felt could ignite into full-blown misery, Clarice extinguished it with her uncanny finesse. "Don't sweat it," she said. "We've all been there with Ann. She's such a pro she could talk a leopard out of his spots."

In the light of that statement, the obvious question that I had previously ignored floated to surface. If every employee of GWS started at the bottom, why would they have run the ad for a management position in the first place?

I knew I had been duped, and might have looked for another job if working beside Clarice hadn't already become such an attractive prospect. I stayed. Clarice taught me the ins and outs of customer service, and filled me in on office politics. She was a year younger than I, but seemed eons wiser. When I pointed that out, she waved me off.

"I have more experience, that's all. I skipped college and spent those four years here, learning the hard way. We each have a calling in life. You'll move up one day and improve working conditions for the rest of us. I'll be here to share my experience and train the best customer service reps anyone could ask for."

I wasn't sure I understood Clarice. "Why do you stay here?"

"For the customers," she said. "They pay a small fortune for water and sewers, so they deserve good customer service. I deliver that." She shrugged. "It's a tough job, but somebody's gotta do it."

I shook my head. "Don't try to distract me with clichés, Clarice. This is much worse than a tough job. It's a thankless job. Why?"

"Don't blow me off without thinking this through," she asked. "Seems like everybody wants to be something important or fancy – a doctor, or lawyer, or CEO, or movie star."

"Careful," I warned. "You just ticked off roll call for my family." I hoped this didn't mean she was one of those reverse snobs who look down their noses at anyone who had more or set higher goals, without bothering to get to know them first.

As if reading my mind, she came back quickly. "I admire those people, if they're doing what they were called to do and not just there for the money. And, so long as they treat others who aren't like them with respect. My point is, every job is important in the big picture. A thousand piece jigsaw puzzle isn't complete if the dog ate one measly little piece. The world needs customer service and floor cleaners."

I agreed. Her clarification resolved my fear that she was a snob but left me unsure about my own ranking on the snob meter. In my search for ways to understand Clarice's reason for wanting to stay in what seemed like a crap job, I realized it was equally important to me that she at least confirm some understanding of my side. And then I wondered how ugly it was for me to consider that we there were sides and we weren't on the same one.

"So you understand that it has nothing to do with loyalty to the company?" she asked. "It's all about me caring enough about the customers? Helping them makes me happy in this job."

I understood in principle, but couldn't relate by wanting that for myself. The pleading tone in her voice extracted my nod.

It didn't take long for me to notice that a suspicious number of GWS customers came to the office to make payments instead of mailing their checks or paying on the internet, and that they were disappointed when I took their payment instead of Clarice. They brought her brownies, pictures of grandchildren, knitted scarfs, and flowers from their yards – tokens of friendship – and she flashed them with her big smiles in return.

Clarice McDaniels plucked fulfillment from seemingly bare experiences. Maybe I couldn't relate to her career goals, but I knew I wanted that plucking ability for myself. I had things to learn from this girl.

For months, I saw Clarice only during working hours. She never mentioned any outside activities, and I didn't pry. When I got used to the sound of snot in her voice and the slurping in her smile, I looked forward to eating lunch with her every day, even if she chose not to share the rest of her life with me. The manager in me – strictly book learning and no experience – knew we shouldn't have the same lunch schedule. But as long as Ann was willing to send her secretary to cover our windows while we were away, I kept my opinion to myself and looked forward to the time we shared.

Clarice took me to all the different cafes, delis and fast food restaurants, in the neighborhood and introduced me to the regulars in each. Whether in the halls at GWS, on the streets in the neighborhood, or in restaurants, I noticed two things remained consistent. Clarice had a kind word for everyone, and people seemed to love her. And Clarice ordered the least expensive item on the menu.

Finally, I decided we knew each other well enough that I could invite her to do something outside of work without appearing to intrude beyond the boundaries she protected. I asked Clarice to join me for the annual end of summer pool party and barbecue at my parents' house, with a compound motive. Most importantly, I enjoyed her company and wanted to extend our friendship beyond work. Also, I thought Clarice would make a delightful addition to my mother's stuffy guest list, perhaps turning on a few lights that had been out for years. And, selfishly, I knew my mother wouldn't nag me in front of a new friend.

Clarice blew me off at first. Then, when I pressed gently, she teased about checking her date book for conflicts, and making me promise there'd be no paparazzi. Eventually, she accepted.

"My family is more the keg-of-beer-everybody-bring-a-dish type than the poolside barbecue," Clarice said. "Before I trudge in wearing my overalls, with my famous baked beans in one hand and a thermos of sweet tea in the other, and embarrass both of us, you'd better tell me about house rules and dress codes."

I wanted to lie, unfairly assuming that Clarice would be as shallow as most of the friends I had chosen before her and judge me by my family. But she deserved the truth, even if it meant she would change her mind about going to the party.

Half-ashamed, I tried to apologize for my family even though they had really done nothing wrong. "My mother will hire valets to park cars on their side lawn, caterers to prepare and serve the food, and bartenders to mix and serve drinks. A disk jockey will play music – usually elevator music I'm afraid - and a certified lifeguard will protect the pool. If she thinks about it in time, she might provide heated towels."

"Okay," Clarice said. "That settles it for me. I'm not bringing the baked beans. What should I wear?"

I advised Clarice honestly. "I think you should start a new trend in this crowd. Wear a smile and no one there will notice what else you're wearing.

~~~

Clarice rejected my offer to pick her up so she could ride to the party with me. I didn't blame her. I figured she wanted to have her own car available so she could leave if the party bored her, or if she found she hated the strangers she had agreed to spend the day with. But Clarice gave a much different reason for preferring to drive her own car.

"And miss my first opportunity to have a valet open the door of my Escort and help me out? Not on your life, Girlfriend. That sounds so romantic. I aim to make the most of this. I'll feel like a movie star."

"In that case," I told her, "I hope Mother hired Rodrigo again this year. He'll make your knees so weak you'll need his help to get out of that Escort."

Clarice raised an eyebrow over the top of her glasses and smiled. "Maybe I'll bring a camera."

How well I knew the weak knees Rodrigo caused. I didn't want to get out of my car that year and probably wouldn't have if Dad hadn't come after me.

I sat in the side yard at my parents' house and waited while Rodrigo ran back and forth. He'd park a car and then run back to my Honda, where he sat in the passenger seat and told me his life story in bits and pieces. I wish I could say I hung on to every word, but the truth is I only hung on to the ones I wanted to hear and blocked the others out.

He told me about his parents and four sisters in Columbia who missed him and wrote letters every week. Sometimes it was weeks before he received the letters, but they were what kept him going. I missed having siblings more than I ever had before when he talked about his.

He got excited when he told me he was studying for his MBA and hoped to use his education to help restore economic stability in his country when he returned. And he got sad when he told me about Martina, the girlfriend who married his best friend because she didn't want to wait while Rodrigo came to the United States to study.

I was still trying to figure out how any girl could let this man get away, when Dad opened my car door. He leaned over and acknowledged Rodrigo with a nod, but directed his words at me.

"Your mother is quite concerned about this situation," he warned. "She thinks you are being rude to our guests."

I doubted there was one guest present who missed me. Besides, it was her party and her friends, so they shouldn't expect me to entertain them. I turned to roll my eyes at Rodrigo so he would know I wasn't pleased that my father had interrupted our conversation. He gave me a look that said he understood.

"I think you should come back and join the party now," Dad said. "You can talk to your friend later."

Rodrigo said that was right, we could talk later. Those were the words I hung on to. All day I thought about him, and how exciting it was to meet a man with real goals.

Quite concerned wasn't exactly how I would have described my mother's reaction. Dad minimized her fury more than usual with that statement.

She pulled me into an upstairs bedroom on the front side of the house, closed the door, and still whispered, as though the world might stop turning if any of her friends heard what she had to say. I embarrassed her by sitting in the car when we had guests. I should have been helping her entertain. The lecture took a good ten minutes of her time away from the guests she was so concerned about, and in all that time she never said the truth. She was embarrassed because I socialized with the hired help.

Rodrigo asked for my phone number when he brought my car back that evening, but he never used it. I told myself Mother must have sent a death threat with his paycheck or something, but I know better.

That was three years before, but I thought it was possible that he was still around. I didn't know how likely it was that he would still be parking cars for a living, but for Clarice's sake I hoped he was. Every girl needs to experience a Rodrigo for at least an hour of her life.

I went to the party early in case Mother needed help with last minute preparations. As usual, she didn't need my help because she hired all of the 'best' people.

With caterers, servers, drink mixers and a toilet paper changer swarming my mother's kitchen as though *they* owned the place and I was the outsider, I felt like I was in the way. At least Clarice hadn't come along to witness this circus.

The toilet paper specialist, Mother's regular housekeeper, was a new attraction this year, added because Lois Kampar spent fifteen humiliating minutes drip-drying in the downstairs powder room last year before anyone came to her rescue. I laughed for days, because there was a box of tissue on the vanity the whole time, but mother failed to catch the humor.

Betty visited every bathroom in the house, as well as those outdoors by the pool, to make sure they all started out with a full roll. She would check them all periodically throughout the day to prevent another tragedy such as Lois'.

Thanks to the salsa craze, Mother chose a Latin theme that year. Papier-mâché sombreros, donkeys or llamas – I couldn't tell which – and cholitas made of sticks and string served as party favors and decorations. Although she tried to discourage inside traffic by keeping decorations at a bare minimum inside the house, a ceramic flamenco dancer stood in the center of the service island, watching the circus from behind her fan. Rodrigo would have fit in perfectly at this year's party.

Mother filled two crystal glasses with freshly squeezed lemonade, laced with cranberry juice, handed one to me, and led me to the pool area. Just once, I wanted to use plastic cups and paper plates and pretend it was a real picnic. And maybe one day before I died, she would let me be the leader and choose where I wanted to sit.

In full make-up, a yellow silk wrap-around skirt, and a bikini top, Mother poised herself in a chaise lounge and ordered me into the one beside hers. I listened to her not-so-subtle suggestion that I could have worn something nicer – meaning more like what her friends would wear – than khaki shorts and a white tank top. She reminded me that I was always welcome to change into something of hers.

I tried to summon the courage to share my opinion of her appearance, but accepted my fate as the curator of silenced brainstorms. In my feeble opinion, she looked ridiculous in both make-up and a bathing suit top. If she planned to swim, the make-up was a waste. If she didn't plan to swim, the bikini top was gaudy.

I told her I didn't think I could fit into her fives anymore and vaulted right back onto her good side, tacky clothes and all. I knew she would harass me about diets when the elation wore off, but I'd deal with that when the time came.

"So tell me, Rena, how are you?" That struck me as an odd question from mother to daughter, so I waited for the punch line. It came soon enough.

"We don't see enough of you these days and I was so sure we would be close again when you came back from college."

My brain shorted out with two relative terms to consider in one sentence. Enough. That could mean she thought I was overdressed in my tank top, and she wished I would run up to her closet and change into any one of her many skimpy tops. Or, she may have intended it to imply that I should want to see her more often. I knew it didn't mean she wanted to see me more often, since the only thing stopping her was the fact that she never called or came to visit.

I didn't spend much time on 'close'. Proximity won without discussion.

I looked over at her raised eyebrows and knew she either expected a response, or Marvin screwed up big time on her wax job. My standard response – sorry – slipped out before I thought of anything more creative or less antagonistic than the truth.

Sorry worked well with Mother because she assumed it positioned her on top. I took advantage and announced that I had invited a friend from work while she was still wrapped in the revelry of my 'sorry'.

"Wonderful, Dear. Your friends are always welcome. Is it someone you're dating?"

The temptation was almost too great to pass up. I would have traded my next four paychecks for the nerve to say yes and then watch Mother's face when Clarice walked in. Loyalty to Clarice reined in the urge.

"No, Mother. Clarice is a dear friend."

Something in me wanted to warn mother that Clarice was different, but the fact that the word warn had come to mind stopped me. Clarice deserved so much more than that. My mother, despite what she may think or say privately, would present herself as the perfect hostess, even to Clarice and without warning. I counted on that.

Dad called Mother to the main tent because he didn't know where she wanted the florist to put the palms. A world of nature surrounded the house, but leave it to Mother to order something fake to decorate with.

I escaped to the kitchen to find something stronger than cranberry spiked lemonade to prepare me for the next round.

Chapter 3

Mother's cousin had me pinned against the fence recounting the ribbons her show dogs had won over the past year when Clarice arrived, fashionably late and scantily dressed. She carried herself into this mob of strangers with an air that commanded respect. My first thought was that she was stunning and the second was that should have been Mother's daughter.

I waved so Clarice would find me easily, and so Mother's cousin would wrap up her description of Muffin's perfect performance. Clarice waved back, delivering a somewhat reserved, lips-stretched-over-the-teeth smile that I hoped was a nervous reaction and not a sign that she planned to spend the rest of the day trying to hide her teeth.

Relieved when the cousin noticed my wave and I had a justifiable reason to extract myself from the conversation permanently, I excused myself and practically ran across the lawn to greet my guest.

"You look adorable in that dress." I said as I hugged her, forgetting that she was a coworker and not one of Mother's demonstrative friends. Clarice returned a full, slurping smile, but extracted herself quickly from the hug.

The compliment was actually an understatement. Gorgeous legs and more than ample cleavage framed the tiny, black-and-white-striped sundress I was shocked to see Clarice wear. The dress, combined with platform sandals and spiked hair, offered credibility to anyone who assumed that she added the rhinestone glasses as a fashion statement. I considered it a brilliant move on her part but immediately wondered if this was the real Clarice and maybe the glasses *were* a fashion statement that had been restricted by the stuffy GWC dress code.

I stepped back to look her over again. "Clarice, where do you leave that body when you come to work? I had no idea you looked like this under the baggy clothes you wear to work."

"Don't try to draw my attention away, Girlfriend. You're in big trouble. I had my mind fixed on Rodrigo and got Gretchen instead."

I placed both hands on my chest and feigned a broken heart. "Rodrigo must have changed professions. He's probably busy rescuing his country from financial ruin by now, and much too busy to park cars."

"It's just as well," she said. "I like you too much to risk our friendship fighting over some man who probably doesn't deserve us anyway."

I told Clarice I should take her to meet my parents, initially wondering what my impression of them would be if I could meet them for the first time that day. Without twenty-four years of history, would they look the same to me? Later, I wondered if Clarice had noticed how differently my parents had reacted – both to her and to me – admitting to myself that I had spent my entire life wondering why they ended up together.

We found mother sitting under a fan in a small tent, totally immersed in a legal discussion with one of her partners. Clarice didn't appear to notice, but I recognized the subtle distaste in Mother's expression when she finally looked up and saw us standing beside her table. I saw it only because I was familiar with *the look*.

The look had introduced its repugnant self to me when Sissy Eickle arrived at my eighth birthday party. Mother's face hardened and she left Sissy standing in the foyer while she pulled me into the pantry for the inquisition.

"She wasn't on the guest list and she does not have an invitation," Mother said.

"I asked her, Mama. She was sad because she didn't receive an invitation." I was so sure my mother would understand. "So I told her where to come."

"We aren't prepared for her. There are only enough chairs for invited guests."

"She can share my seat, Mama."

"Absolutely not. The child just got over head lice."

Another seat miraculously appeared for Sissy, at the opposite end of the table from me.

The look came out again that day when I opened Sissy's gift – a bottle of bubbles and a picture of me that she had drawn on construction paper. It came out again when I brought (her words) *the flamer* home for Thanksgiving weekend because he wasn't welcome at his own family gathering, and it stayed on Mother's face the entire time she launched the Rodrigo lecture. Although it didn't come often, *the look* was unmistakable and I resented it more every time I saw it.

Mother tried to cover by winking at Clarice, but she continued her legal train of thought before breaking away for introductions. I knew that put Clarice in her place, even if she didn't.

When she finally got to us, Mother used her sweetest voice and it affected my gag reflexes the same as a tablespoon of sugar might have if I tried to swallow it. "Clarice dear, welcome. I hope Rena is taking good care of you and showing you where to find everything."

Clarice smiled, and apologized to mother's partner for interrupting their conversation. He said no apology was necessary; they probably shouldn't have been discussing business at the party anyway. Mother apparently mistook that as a hint to resume the conversation since she dismissed us with quick hugs and returned where she had left off with him.

Dad was at the far end of the property setting up the volleyball net. He tried to get a game going every year but, each year, fewer of their friends humored him by playing.

He stopped what he was doing when he saw us coming and greeted Clarice with his big smile and a handshake.

"I'm happy to meet you." His voice and body language were sincere and friendly. "Please make yourself at home and let me know if there's anything I can do to help you girls have a better time." He pointed at the framework he had been constructing. "We're going to have a volleyball game later. Do you play, Clarice?"

I stopped him. "Dad, you just met her. If you start begging this soon it'll ruin your image."

"Think about it," he said to Clarice. "It's great exercise. Come back when the net is up and I'll beat both of you at once."

"Poor Dad, he's beginning to thinks volleyball is a two person game," I explained as I took her to see my old playhouse before we returned to the party scene. "He can't ever get full teams together any more. I guess he hasn't noticed yet that he and his friends are getting old."

We made our way back to the hub. Using two fingers on each hand as pointers, and staccato motions, I mocked an airline hostess. "Food and air-conditioning are housed in the humongous tent on the left, music and drinks in the medium-sized tent across from it. For those approaching the senior years, we have card tables set up in the small tent to the right, and if you're boring beyond belief, you may enjoy the quiet tent furthest to the back, where mother is still boring poor Phil to tears."

I turned the other direction. "Bathrooms are located at both ends of the pool, and disbursed efficiently throughout the house. If you need assistance in that area, contact Betty, the tall, gray-haired lady running around with a jumbo pack of Charmin under her arm."

Clarice threw her hand up to cover her mouth and chortle, and her purse slid off her arm.

"I apologize for being such a rotten hostess," I said. "I don't get into this party stuff the way my mother does. I'm more casual and prefer smaller gatherings where everyone knows each other and takes care of themselves. Come on,"

I said, leading her toward the house. "I'll show you where to drop your purse."

Clarice looked around the lavish kitchen in disbelief. Her mouth may have been agape, I really couldn't tell. "You actually grew up in this house?" she asked. "It looks like a museum or something. No offense, I've just never seen a home this big."

"No offense taken," I assured her. "I agree with you. It also feels more like a museum than a home. They allowed me to look but not touch, walk but not run, and reminded me constantly to keep my voice at a level acceptable in a museum or library. Want the whole tour?"

Her eyes widened. "You bet. I love museums."

We roamed through the gargantuan display of wealth mixed with garish, snickering at the more predictable symbolisms, like the chandelier in the foyer, the grand piano, and grandfather clock, necessary only to people living a generation behind.

Clarice laughed out loud, wiping the corners of her mouth with her thumb and index finger. "What's the purpose of the chandelier? When would anyone need that much light to find their way in?"

"Better yet," I asked in return, "when would fifty people arrive at once, making the stupid foyer necessary in the first place? I lived in a space smaller than that for four years, and shared it with a roommate." I laughed so hard that I had to hold my sides to keep from doubling over.

Clarice stopped laughing. The change was as abrupt as the silence that would startle dancers if the stereo cord were suddenly unplugged. I delivered the same startled reaction, and stopped in my tracks. I couldn't read what I saw in her face but quickly decided not to mention the peculiar silence in case it had something to do with slurping or drool control.

In an effort to lighten the mood again, I went back into tour guide role. "If you will be so kind as to follow me, we have one last exhibit, appropriately titled 'Rena's Room'."

"'Rena's Room, As Seen Through Charlotte's Eyes' would be more appropriate," I corrected, before opening the door to Mother's masterpiece. The few things that might have reflected my personality - the picture Sissy Eickle had given me for my birthday, my Michael Jackson posters, and my CD collection – left when I did and never had to stay in a closet again.

Clarice gasped when I opened the door, unveiling a wonderland that might have made Alice weep with envy.

"Rena, were you ever this prissy? I can't picture that."

I shook my head, grateful to her for asking.

She ran across the cotton-candy-pink carpet and plunged, giggling, into the pile of ruffled pillows on the queen-sized canopy bed. "You must have felt like a princess in here."

"Keep in mind," I urged, "that I was eighteen-years-old when I left here. I felt more like the pea than the princess. I didn't bring a friend to my room after sixth grade. Their rooms grew up as they did, and reflected their own taste instead of their mothers' childhood dreams. I knew they'd tease me about this."

Clarice got serious again. "No slumber parties? No sleepovers, even with your best friend?"

"Not in this house. I stayed over at my friends' houses often, but never asked them here."

She walked around the room with her hands clasped behind her back, carefully inspecting the furniture and the drapes and paintings. She finally conceded. "It's obscene. But I still can't believe you'd rather fork over your hard earned GWS money for rent than live here. Girlfriend, are you crazy? You could run around this place for days without bumping into another living soul."

"I hate to disappoint you, but I think you have the wrong impression," I said. Clarice needed a few more minutes with my mother – then she'd understand. "Mother would have me back under radar surveillance within minutes and there'd be no running in the museum. Then she'd hone in and follow me, every step. And she isn't satisfied just knowing where I am, she feels the need to control my thoughts as well."

"She loves you," Clarice said.

"She smothers me," I corrected.

Accepting that both of us had broken from the light, laughing mood, I dropped down to sit cross-legged on the carpet, and patted the floor beside me. It was a position I learned to love as a child, when I sat down there to look at the treasures I kept hidden under my bed. "Sit down," I said, "and let me explain my interpretation of this complex exhibit."

Clarice joined me on the floor and we rested our backs against the bed. I wished I hadn't promised a horror story because I could tell she wanted to get into the theme of the room and talk about Barbie Dolls and party dresses. "In Mother's eyes, I will always be a child because she selfishly views everything in terms of how it relates to her," I said. "She tries to be generous. The amount she donates to charity in a year is greater than my salary, and she spends countless hours delivering food to shelters, and barely used clothes to church groups. I'm not so callous that I won't recognize her effort. But in the end, it's all about Charlotte and how her friends will praise her – or how she can use the donations to offset taxes – or how her actions will be picked up by the next person who writes a news clip or bio on her."

"It sounds like a win-win situation to me," Clarice said. "Everyone comes out ahead."

I laid my head back on the bed, wondering which of us missed the point. We sat that way, in silence for a while and then went back outside and took leaning positions again, this time over the deck railing while we reoriented ourselves to the party. The guests in our age range, who generally waited until the parents had finished small talk and had a few drinks before they came, had started to trickle in. A small group of them had taken over the music tent and were cheering Justin Forbes on as he did his

Ricky Martin impersonation, which had become an annual event.

The pool was crowded, mostly with people who owed their great bodies to Justin's father, Larry, our resident plastic surgeon. Larry sat on the side of the pool admiring his work. His wife, seethed in jealousy, drank herself into oblivion in the bar tent. If this year followed tradition, someone would carry her inside to a bed before long.

Dad the neurosurgeon, and Dan Jackson the cardiologist, paired off against George Downs the orthodontist, and Rob Rodes the anesthesiologist, in an attempt at a volleyball game. I hoped more people would join them because they seemed to be chasing the ball more often than they volleyed it, and wearing out fast.

Clarice finally broke the silence. "I'll never keep all of these names straight. Are all of your parents' friends doctors?"

"No, some are attorneys. And remember, these are Mother's friends, and people who work with Dad that she wants to impress. I'm not sure he actually considers them friends. Choose your poison, Clarice. Where do you want to settle, or would you prefer to mingle? Did you bring a bathing suit?"

Clarice didn't bring a suit but said she wanted to sit by the pool and dip her feet in.

"That sounds great to me. But I can't promise those overgrown kids won't splash us," I warned.

I spread a towel out on the concrete and Clarice and I sat on the side of the pool with our feet in the water. I introduced Clarice to the plastic crowd and wondered how long it would take before someone asked if Larry did her boobs.

Janice, wife of George the orthodontist and owner of the largest implants in the pool, forfeited her chaise lounge and descended on Clarice like a vulture. I recognized the dollar signs in her eyes, and she must have seen the warning in mine, because she quickly went into a review of a story she had seen on Good Morning America, without mentioning her husband's occupation.

Mother called me to help her wipe up the kitchen floor. In all her perfect planning, she had forgotten to hire a floor dryer. Amazing. Clarice told me to go ahead, she'd be fine.

"I can't believe people tracked through here with wet feet." Mother pouted with the new lip Larry had sold her. "The reason we have bathrooms and changing rooms by the pool is because we don't want wet people inside the house. You'd think that would be obvious."

She handed me a towel so I could wipe while she continued, breaking her rant only when Cheryl Rodes came in to reapply her lipstick in the dining room mirror. Mid-sentence, my mother changed her personality from raving lunatic to placating lush. Too bad Clarice missed the performance; it was bound to be more entertaining than Janice's human-interest story.

On hands and knees, I dried most of the twelve-square-feet of ceramic tiles in the kitchen and decided I had done enough. "I need to get back to Clarice," I said. "She doesn't know anyone."

"Rena, dear, what's wrong with that poor girl?"

"There's nothing wrong with her that I've noticed," I said, shoving the wet towel in her hand before I walked out.

I went back to the pool, relieved to find that Dad had taken my place next to Clarice. I knew he wouldn't have let Janice get too far if she tried to promote George's orthodontic skills.

Dad smiled. "It's about time you made your way back. Clarice and I were just about to get in the food line without you. The pork is finally done, and doesn't it smell heavenly?"

It did. I apologized for leaving Clarice so long. She said not to worry, she had a great conversation with Dad. I wondered whose secrets he pumped her for – hers or mine. The difference between Dad's snooping and Mother's, and what made me resent it less, is that he never used anything he learned against me.

Clarice stayed until dusk, eventually leaving me to mingle on her own. She looked more at home than I felt, especially when she finally settled in with Justin's fan club. Even though my parents forced me to associate with these kids most of my life, I didn't consider any of them close friends and I only saw them at functions like this one. I had little in common with these people and believed I would have less in common with them as I grew to know Clarice better. Why was she cozying up to them?

When Clarice was ready to leave, I walked out front to wait with her while Gretchen retrieved the Escort. She thanked me for inviting her and said she had a great time. I thanked her for coming, and for helping me have a good time despite myself.

Clarice looked away, staring into the row of blue spruces that separated our house from the one next to it. She spoke just before Gretchen pulled up with the car. "Do you mind if I ask you a personal question, Rena?"

"Ask away," I told her. "I'll answer any questions you have."

"Did you notice how many times today someone said you look great? Every time we walked up to someone different, they said 'you're looking great Rena', or 'great hair cut Rena', or something like that."

"I wasn't counting. They say whatever they think other people expect to hear, Clarice. They don't even mean it." If that was her personal question, it was a strange one. Either she wanted to test my math skills, or there was more to come.

More came. Without looking at me, she asked another question. "How does that feel?"

Chapter 4

I thought, because my parents had introduced me to some new, exciting corner of the world on each of our semi-annual vacations, that made me worldly. I met interesting people, and experienced holidays and festivals in different cultures. I knew how to find my way through airports and how to order a meal or request the ladies' room in five languages. What more could there possibly be in order to qualify?

In contrast, I experienced what I considered the formidable side of life; the things I believed helped me to develop character and wisdom. I watched drugs and alcohol ravage the minds and bodies of some of my childhood friends, as well as some of the new ones I met in college. I held their hands, smelled their puke and sweat, heard their cries, and allowed myself to see what their parents wouldn't.

I rebelled strongly in college, doing as little schoolwork as I possibly could without compromising the free ride Dad offered for very little in return. I partied, and tried to experience a little of everything my parents had warned me against, maybe even a few things they hadn't thought to mention.

I decorated my half of the dorm in borderline sleaze to obliterate all memories of the princess bedroom I left behind at the museum, and refused to clean it until the dorm monitor threatened me with expulsion or a phone call to my parents. My clothes and books, and the picture Sissy Eickle drew for my birthday present, lived in the sleaze, but most nights I shared a bed with Keith Warner, or Scott Moran, or Matthew what's-his-name, in various off-campus apartments.

I had seen starving children in third world countries, with their hands held out. Old friends had disappointed me and new ones fell short of my expectations. Keith broke my heart. Matthew cleaned out my bank account and ran Dad's credit card up to a limit that nearly got me cut off. And my roommate, Lori Zeller, wrecked my car.

But nothing in my vast collection of worldly experiences prepared me for the devastating aftermath of Clarice's question, *how does that feel* or my pathetic answer to it, *generic.*

I wouldn't blame Clarice if she hated me for that answer and refused to ever speak to me again. At least generic isn't a relative term; it's absolute. Absolutely the most meaningless answer possible to the question *how does that feel*, rating right up there with *because I said so* as an answer to the question *why.* It was obvious to me that I should never have children if this was the best I could do with difficult questions.

I kicked the coffee table away from the couch and wilted to the floor. Hard times called for hard surfaces.

I contributed nothing to the atmosphere or to my comfort, no light or sound, no popcorn and soda, and certainly no TV or computer. Maybe, subconsciously, I believed I didn't deserve comfort; or maybe I thought a void offered more protection than complete awareness. I was too filled with self-loathing to even consider getting drunk so I didn't have to think or feel.

Splinters of light flashed in the corner of the room as the headlights of passing cars slipped through the crack between the blinds and window frame, reminding me that my mother told me I needed to hang drapes and she might possibly have known what she was talking about. The sporadic light also brought back memories of sleepless nights, when I was too lazy to wrestle the remote out from under Matthew so I watched the TV screen cast similar flashes on Matthew's bedroom wall.

On one such night, I turned toward the screen and watched a late night journalist profile a young man who had lost both arms in a farm machinery accident. The man proudly demonstrated how adeptly he had mastered the use of bilateral prosthetics. For the whole world to see, or at least the insomniacs, he tied his shoes and necktie, and cut a piece of roast beef with a steak knife.

I felt sorry for the guy as well as for his bubbly little wife who surely never thought she would be married to a man without arms. He lost his job and gave up the basketball team, although he intended to play again one day. She believed in him and looked on with pride as he demonstrated his skills.

I decided I couldn't take any more and dove for the remote when they cut away to show a therapist preparing a stump to be fitted with an artificial limb, not caring if I woke Matthew or how angry that might make him. I wasn't sure if it was farmer's stump, or even if it was an arm, because I couldn't look. I flipped the station to find something less gory.

At two o'clock in the morning, with only basic cable, my choices included the armless man, an infomercial for a juicer, a replay of the all night news program that I had already seen twice, and a western in black and white. I kept flipping, hoping I had missed a better option.

The armless man caught my attention again during a later turn, and I stopped flipping. He said, initially, at the moment his arms were severed, he hadn't felt any pain. He didn't even know his arms were missing until he tried to push himself up from the facedown position he had landed in, and found he wasn't moving. He looked down to see why his arms were so weak and that's when he realized they were gone.

I thought that was amazing. He was a lucky man - lucky because he didn't feel the pain, not lucky because he lost his arms.

Then, just when I decided the story was interesting after all, he slammed me with bad news. As his nerves recovered from the trauma, he started to feel the pain. Not only did he experience pain at the site where his arms had been severed, he continued to ache and itch in the parts of the arms that were missing. Unbelievable.

Phantom pain they called it. It was part of the healing process.

Eventually, his pain improved and he calloused his stumps enough to be able to tolerate prosthetics. For the serious insomniac, they showed another clip of him changing his son's diaper.

Matthew-what's-his name -- six beers past his limit and a card short in his deck – had been listening to the last part and he laughed hysterically at the whole idea of phantom pain. He said he couldn't believe the man didn't have any more pride than to make a fool of himself on television changing a diaper. Rather than argue with Matthew, or hate him for being such a jerk, I drove back to the dorm and lay awake imagining how it would feel to have cramps in fingers that weren't there.

The phantom pain concept haunted me for days. In the middle of an accounting class I suddenly wondered what I would do if my brain commanded my hand to scratch an itch on my nose and there was no hand available to do the job.

I finally realized that there was a message in remembering the armless man at this time; pain accompanies healing. If I could survive the pain and wait for the calluses to form, I would be able to replace what I had lost, or at least tolerate a facsimile of it. I cheated at first. Anxious for pain to replace empty, I sat in the same position until my right leg and butt cheek fell asleep, and then I refused to move. But nothing healed. I still felt empty.

Sometime before daybreak, during that hazy period when you can make out the objects in the room by the light of the heavy film that ushers in the sun, my phantom pain kicked in. A mental image of Clarice's naïve eyes staring out at the blue spruces through rhinestone glasses assailed me like a relentless itch that I couldn't reach. Clarice, the wise one, asking me for one simple answer – and all I had to offer her was an immature *generic*.

I looked down to see why I was too weak to move, and discovered that I had lost my claim to worldliness. My answer to Clarice's question was the best answer I could offer her because everything in my life was generic.

I had seen the world, not experienced it. I spent the summers associating with the other tourists who shared our first rate hotels, not staying with and talking to the people who lived in those countries we visited.

True to character, Mother used the residents of our vacation spots to serve her own purpose. She asked Dad to take pictures which often showed up in local stories about her, not them. As she opened her purse to hand out the charity money, she reminded me how fortunate I was to have been born her daughter. "Their mommies and daddies can't afford to buy them food or toys, so they have to beg for coins from strangers in the street. Those poor little children."

I smelled someone else's puke, in someone else's car or home. I didn't know how it felt to clean up my father's puke off the bathroom floor, or to puke my own guts up, or to withdraw from a heroin addiction. I lost things that were replaceable, or forgettable. And I knew how it felt to hear compliments – both generic and authentic.

When the real pain set in, I decided the hard surface wasn't necessary anymore and curled up on the couch to mourn my loss and develop my calluses. I grieved.

Emily Post or Ann Landers or some such person owned the compliments Clarice heard me receive at the party. I knew that, and wrongly assumed she would. The Cheryl Rodes and Janice Downs of the world memorized their plastic compliments long before they started buying their plastic bodies. If any of them had looked closely enough to remember what I was wearing or how I truly looked at the party, they were on the phone tonight gossiping about how tacky the khaki shorts were and how wide they made my ass look, and speculating the cause of bags under my eyes regardless of the compliments they had offered to my face.

Clarice probably didn't understand because she came from an honest family and didn't have to deal with people she couldn't trust.

~~~

Mr. and Mrs. Ash from across the hall returned from their after-church brunch fighting the same battle they had every Sunday since I moved into the apartment. Obviously, he was never going to stop piling bacon and sausage on his plate, and she intended to deliver the same cholesterol sermon until the day his clogged arteries finally (her words) *killed him dead* and proved her the winner of this battle.

On cue, their door opened again ten minutes after the first slam and Mr. Ash came out to walk Bango, the barking beagle, until Mrs. Ash calmed down. Since I was wide awake for all of this, I know it was at least noon – twenty-eight hours after I got up on Saturday to go to my parents' party – before I dozed off.

Mother called and woke me again at four. I wasn't alert. I wasn't nice.

The fatigue and rasp in my voice escaped her cognizance, and she didn't stop to ask trivial, appropriate, lead-in questions like *did I wake you* or *are you okay*. She launched straight into her spiel.

"Rena, I've been on the phone all morning making arrangements. I have the most wonderful news. I've prepared a complete make-over for your poor little friend, Clarissa." I imagined how pleased she must have been with herself.

"Clarice. Mother, her name is Clarice. And regardless of her size, she isn't a little girl. She's my age."

I stretched my eyes and shook my head in an attempt to wake enough to grasp the meaning behind my mother's announcement. It occurred to me that she and I had very different perceptions of wonderful, and hers tended to send my blood pressure soaring into dangerous heights.

As the waking fog slowly cleared, the phone felt heavier in my hand and the information coming through it became harder to digest. I switched the phone to the other ear, as if that would somehow reverse what I thought I had heard, and probed for details.

"I hope you didn't book her on some cheap talk show," I said. Although I couldn't imagine my mother knowing about daytime television talk show makeovers, it was possible one of her friends had suggested it. "You'll have to cancel. You can't humiliate Clarice."

"Oh for heaven's sake, Rena. Give me credit for being a little above that sort of thing. That poor little girl is a complete mess and we have friends who can help her, discretely, not on national television. Isn't that why you invited her to the barbecue in the first place?"

I switched to the other hand again, too shaken to respond.

"Janice talked George into starting to work on that little girl's mouth without the customary down payment. He offered to work out a payment plan appropriate to her income, even it if takes twenty years for her to pay him off. You know what a tightwad George is, so this is quite an offer. Isn't that nice?"

I paced, still too upset to speak and too sleepy to digest. Concentrating as hard as I could, I thought back over the party. If I counted the introduction in the quiet tent and added a second for each time Mother had accidentally caught Clarice in her peripheral vision, she didn't spend a full minute looking at her. How could she possibly determine that Clarice was a mess and arrange a makeover?

"Dad said he'll pay for contact lenses, or at least new frames – something more stylish and flattering. And I want to take her to see Marvin. He wasn't available this morning, of course, but I know he'll cooperate. Did you notice the gel in her hair? That poor little girl couldn't even plaster that cut in place. Marvin is a miracle worker. I know he can do something, even though her hair is already too short for her face."

"Mother!" I shouted into the phone. "Please. Stop. Clarice is fine just the way she is. Leave her alone."

Mother summoned her Oscar-winning victim's tone. "I don't understand you, Rena. I try to do something nice to help your poor little friend and not only are you too stubborn to acknowledge the trouble I've gone to, you act as though I've done something wrong."

I wanted to ask if she adopted me. This woman and I didn't resemble the same species, much less the same DNA. Her repeated use of the phrase *poor little friend* exposed the underlying significance of this makeover. My mother didn't want to admit that Clarice was my friend. The *little* implied a lot in this case, and I'm sure she used it with her friends to imply that Clarice was my project, not my friend.

I considered the possibility that I just might hate my mother.

Mother knew it would be easier to change my *poor little friend* than it would be to control me, hence the makeover. She had a lot of nerve calling Clarice poor. I believed Clarice owned things Mother never would, because those things couldn't be purchased at the mall. Poor Mother. I wished I could tell her that, but one of the things she didn't own was a clue, so it would only hurt her feelings and get me nowhere.

I changed directions. "Mother, I believe your intentions are commendable, and I appreciate the time you devoted to this cause. But it isn't necessary. Thanks anyway."

She sniffed, probably hoping I would feel guilty for reducing my proud mother to tears, and condemn myself to a lifetime of compliance. I might have, a few months before, or under different circumstances. But this wasn't about me, so I didn't have that option. This was about Clarice and I wouldn't risk her pride to indulge my mother's conniption fit.

Resolved to hold my own, I proceeded as carefully as I could, hoping she would understand and let me go back to sleep. "I don't think you have seen the full scope of this situation, Mother. Clarice is an extremely proud person. And she fixes her hair that way on purpose. She likes it that way. Actually, gelled spikes are very much in style – ask Marvin - or watch a few music videos."

"Rena, the crazy hair thing may very well be a fad, but you'll never convince me that she likes those hideous glasses, or that she wouldn't want her bite to be corrected if given the opportunity. I don't believe anyone would volunteer to walk through life with bucked teeth. Surely you don't believe that's how she wants to look. Besides, having a bite that badly misaligned isn't even healthy. That's probably why she's so thin."

"Of course she would like to fix her teeth," I shot back. "And I would like to be two inches taller." Did I know that about Clarice? Did I know she would like to fix her teeth?

"No," I corrected, "I assume, as you do, that she would like to fix her teeth, and maybe have new glasses. I can promise you, however, whatever changes she makes, she wants to do it on her own."

My blood pressure and temper leveled off. "Mother, Clarice has developed her self-esteem around this appearance, so you'll wound her deeply if you attack it. She likes herself this way. She understands who she is, how she feels, and how she reached this point in her life. You ought to talk to her once. You'd be amazed at how secure she is. Changing anything about her might upset everything she knows. I'm not sure she would want that."

Mother graced me with one of the backhanded compliments that made me dislike her. "Have you been studying psychology, Rena? What you just said made very good sense."

It did make sense, and that surprised me as much as it surprised my mother. Where had it come from? I thought I was blowing off steam – talking out my ass, as Dad would say. But I made very good sense. And Mother noticed. And I still wasn't satisfied.

Before I patted myself on the back, she dropped the other shoe.

"Or are you just parroting what Clarice's counselors have told her?"

"I haven't studied psychology, and I doubt seriously that Clarice has ever seen a psychologist, or that she would share the details of her sessions with me if she had. Mother, I know very little about Clarice's life outside of work because she is a very private person. She shares her beliefs and her wisdom, without details. Knowing that about her, I believe she would be offended if you pry into her life and try to change her."

"Very well, then." Mother sounded defeated. "I won't try to help."

I thought I was off the hook, but she didn't even take time to inhale before she transferred her concern from Clarice to me.

"Have you been seeing anyone, Rena?"

"I see lots of people, Mother. I'm a customer service representative, remember? People stand in line some days to see me, and I see them right back."

She huffed in my ear. "I don't think I like the people you have been seeing if they've caused you to have this attitude."

Where had my mother been the last ten years? If anything, my attitude had improved in recent months. She should thank my new friend for her influence instead of making unfair assumptions about her.

"Apparently you want to keep your life private also, even from your mother. Fine. But I'm disappointed that you feel that way."

I couldn't win with her. "There's nothing to tell you, Mother. I go to work every day, and then I come home. I find something to eat, read, watch television, and play on the computer. Once in a while, I visit Rachel or Jen. I saw a movie last week. I'm not hiding anything from you, there just isn't anything to tell."

"Aren't you lonely?" Her tone was even.

"No, I'm not lonely. I like my life."

That satisfied her, at least temporarily. She let me go so she could call her friends back to tell them I wasn't gracious enough to accept their charity on behalf of my *poor little friend*.

I turned my phone off and went to bed.

Chapter 5
(Clarice)

Excitement took over every cell of my body, scrubbing off the last remnants of self-control I could lay claim to. I drove with one eye on the road and the other darting around, on the lookout for police cars, which increased in volume the closer I got to my side of town. My Cinderella account couldn't afford a speeding ticket, and Emily was more than likely pacing like a watchdog because I was so late already.

Although I needed every red cent in there, the Cinderella account represented more than the actual dollar amount reported on the quarterly statements. The balance swung like a pendulum, never dipping below the fifty dollar limit the bank set and seldom getting back up to my all-time three hundred dollar high but I tried not to fix too much attention on the numbers. Owning the account proved I had dreams and the courage to go after them. That's what mattered most. It also served as a diary, because I remembered which emergency prompted each of the withdrawals.

The account started in a nasty old orange juice bottle, out of spite against my brothers and now it rested safely in World Banc, where my best friend Emily worked, and where my Dad and brothers couldn't snatch a few cents from it when I wasn't looking. The mean males in my life laughed at me and told everyone I had read Cinderella so many times that I believed a fairy godmother would pop in one day and make me beautiful. Then, their friends would laugh with them.

I hated my brothers for years, and I cried myself to sleep at night wondering if it would really take magic to make me beautiful. Mama said I was already beautiful, and it would take magic to make them nice enough in their hearts to see it. I couldn't have survived a day without Mama.

The bad part about my mother, though, was that she never had much control over the boys. So, she came up with a plan. She called me out back where they wouldn't hear, putting on like she needed me to help her pull up some weeds that were fixing to smother the life right out of her tomato plants.

When I got out there, she fiddled with the tomato plants while she told me what she'd come up with. "Clarice, those boys only want to see you cry. If you make believe you don't care what they say, I think they'll leave you alone and find somebody else to pick on. You'll take every bit of the fun right out of it for them."

The very next morning after she said that, they started in on me at breakfast. Instead of arguing or crying about it, I jumped up from the table, snatched a full bottle of orange juice out of David's hand, and emptied it down the drain. With Mama's sharpest butcher knife, I cut a hole in the foil lid and put it back on, not even taking time to rinse the juice out of the bottle first.

"You're right," I said. "The fairy godmother isn't ever going to come. This will be my Cinderella account." They looked at each other and roared. I pretended I didn't hear and held the bottle in the air. "I'm saving for contact lenses and braces. From here on out, every time you tease me, you have to put a nickel in here."

The boys laughed even harder, knowing I couldn't enforce my rule. Despite their ugliness, I deposited every penny I could get my hands on into the bottle. They'd come in my room at night while I tried to study and shake the bottle, and tease some more. One would ask the other to guess how old I'd be when I finally saved enough money to get beautiful and the other would say something mean.

"I think she'll be so old she'll probably have to buy false teeth instead of braces," David would guess.

Michael would add something like, "And a wheelchair. She'd better start putting dimes in there so she can get one with a motor."

So Mama was wrong about the teasing but at least I didn't care so much what they said as long as I had the sticky coins in the bottle to console me.

I wished my brothers could have seen me at that Boiles barbecue. The only way either one of them would ever be at a party like that was if they were hired to flip the steaks on the grill or set up the beer kegs. They couldn't even park cars, since David lost his license and Michael never bothered to get his.

Adrenaline pumped again when the realization of where I had been came back into focus. I promised Emily every detail of the party as payment for convincing her sister to loan me her new dress and shoes. There was so much to tell that it was going to take the rest of the night to make good on that deal. Truth be known, I could probably have spent the whole night just describing the house.

Emily lived in one of the many row houses on Paine Avenue that Bill Brown bought up and converted into apartments. Parking was a nightmare since there was barely enough room for one car in front of each building and usually two or three drivers moved in. The residents held fast to an unwritten set of rules, and threatened physical damage to any car parked in front of the wrong house. I caught on after a slashed tire that caused a forty-six dollar withdrawal from the Cinderella account.

I blew the horn as I drove past the house, to warn Emily that I was on the way. She ran down the back stairs, through the alley, and up a block to meet me in the St. Leo's church parking lot, and started in with questions before I cut the engine off.

"Did you have fun? Were they nice? How many people were there?"

I slid out of the car and hugged Emily. She jumped up and down like we used to do when we were little girls. Rather than stand there looking stiff as a mannequin while she jumped all over the place, I let go of the regal posture I had practiced all day and jumped with her.

"It was unbelievable, Em. I had more fun than you could ever imagine."

I opened the trunk to get my clothes. The dress and shoes set Emily's sister back two months' worth of babysitting money, so she made me sign an agreement saying I'd buy anything I lost, tore, stained or stretched. I wanted to return her things while they were still in perfect condition because there was no point in me throwing out money on an outfit I'd never wear again.

I changed in the small bedroom Emily shared with her mother and two younger sisters. They had a weird arrangement. Emily's parents were divorced but they still lived in the same house. Her dad shared a room with her brother, and the mother slept in the other bedroom with the girls. Emily said it was a financial arrangement and as long as everyone kept their noses out of each other's business it worked.

"Try to keep it down," Emily warned. "Dad's asleep. But hurry up and tell me everything."

"First of all," I told her, "I wish I could have taken you with me. Second, I think Rena really likes me. She hung out with me most of the day, and she talked to me like a real friend – like you do. I can't wait for you to meet her so we can all be friends."

Emily whispered that she was happy for me. That's the kind of friend she had always been. I took to Emily way back in first grade. I told Mama the first day that I thought Emily was nice enough in her heart to see I was beautiful, the same way she did.

Once I got started, it just came pouring out. "You should have seen the house! Oh my GOD, Emily, you've never seen anything like it in your life, not even on television. I swear, Girlfriend, their house is as big as Horton's Department Store, no exaggeration. And everything in it is unbelievably nice. I couldn't even count the bathrooms. There were four outside by the pool, two for women and two for men."

Emily said she thought that was just a little more than necessary for any family, no matter how big it was, and I agreed. I told her a lot of what they had seemed downright wasteful, but I wasn't going to judge them over it because they treated me as good as they treated anyone else there.

"Some girl named Gretchen parked my car for me and then went to fetch it again when I wanted to leave. They had huge barbecue grills, like the ones the city uses to cook for the whole city when they have the festivals in the park during the summer. Waiters walked around carrying trays full of drinks, and nobody had to pay for anything. Rena's dad is a doctor and her mother is a lawyer, so I guess paying for all of that didn't set them back enough to really hurt them. Can you imagine?"

It felt stuffy in the room, maybe because I was talking so fast, so I slid off of Emily's lower bunk, onto a throw rug covering the tile floor. I patted the floor beside me and asked her to move down there where it was cooler. She moved down beside me and we talked until her mother asked us to please shut up so she could go to sleep, just like she did when we were kids, only I wasn't sleeping over. I had to get home to Mama.

Emily walked me back to St. Leo's to get my car, and I promised I'd come back in the morning to tell her the rest. I still hadn't mentioned the pool or the disk jockey, or how big the tents were.

She walked a few steps toward the house when I remembered something that I couldn't wait until the next day to tell her. I started the car and pulled up next to her at the edge of the parking lot.

"Hey Girlfriend," I called out. "Rena told me I looked adorable in that dress." I wasn't bragging; I knew Emily would be happy to hear that. She gave me a thumbs up to let me know she was.

~~~

Parking, at least, wasn't a problem at home. Each lot came equipped with a thin patch of gravel out front. On even years, provided your name appeared on his list of people whose lot fees were paid up, the park manager pulled up in his rusty pickup truck and his pig of a son climbed out at a snail's pace and shoveled a few replacement rocks on the parking space. He never left enough to make up for what had been driven away between the cracks in tires, or thrown away by Stacey's kid down the road, who had an inclination toward pelting as many of them as he could get his grubby hands on against passing cars. Most of the neighbors knew what he was up to and shooed him off no sooner than he stepped foot on their lot.

I owned the only car in the family since Daddy lost his license for having too many DUIs and his car in a poker game. So, except for the nights when David got pissed and hauled dad's recliner out front, the space was all mine. I pitched a hissy every time I got home and found the chair in my way, and begged him to move it back inside before Daddy sobered up, but secretly that was the one thing I liked about David. He was the only one brave or big enough to give the old sot a taste of his own medicine. Even if he was too drunk to remember it the next day, I took a touch of pleasure in knowing that David got one over on him. The only person in the world who deserved a hard time more than David McDaniels was our father, Frank McDaniels.

I never was exactly a daddy's girl, but I don't remember hating him so much before Mama got sick. Maybe I took on her share of disappointment in him then, too, and summed up with what I already had on my own, it just turned into hatred.

Nobody in the family knew exactly where Daddy got the recliner. We just woke up one morning and found the ugly thing taking up a sizeable portion of the living room, just like his console color TV that he wouldn't let go of even though it was too big and had to be repaired every time we turned around. He told us not to worry ourselves over where the recliner came from, but we did. We asked around, in case he stole it out of a neighbor's trailer, like the barbecue grill he brought home for the July Fourth cookout. We wanted to return it before the police showed up again. But nobody ever claimed the ratty old thing and we were stuck with it

Somebody told David they heard that Daddy picked it up and carted it out of a poker game on account of the guy who owned it didn't have enough cash in his pocket to back up the chips he lost to Daddy. Daddy didn't win often, so he wasn't leaving without something to show for it.

The trailer was dark when I went in except for the pink glow from the lava lamp I left burning in Mama's room. I picked up the habit of turning it on for her when Daddy took up sleeping in the recliner every night. He pitched a fit when I brought it home, insisting that it was a waste of electricity. But he changed his tune when he realized it kept her quiet, sometimes for hours at a time, and that meant he could get some sleep even when he wasn't passed out. A few times, she slept half the night without hollering out at all, and I was willing to bet the Cinderella account it was because the lava lamp soothed her.

I really thought Daddy had nerve to complain in the first place, since he hadn't paid the electric bill in over a year - one of the reasons the pendulum never made it over to three hundred. One by one, he stopped paying for everything when I went to work - lot rental, groceries, and telephone - and I wasn't very happy with the situation but there wasn't any use in fretting over it.

Try as I might, I couldn't figure out any way to take care of Mama alone or I would have moved out and took her with me. I supported both of us as it was, and in some ways the rest of the family, too. But I needed help getting Mama in and out of the tub, and to the car when she had to go to the doctor.

The boys watched over her, to some degree anyway, while I worked and when I went to the Laundromat and grocery store on Saturday. If I made her a plate lunch, or left a sandwich prepared, one of them would carry it back there to her on a tray at lunchtime. They'd even help her eat, so long as their friends didn't come around to distract them. Once, I came home and found her lunch still in the refrigerator. I threatened to tell Daddy, so it never happened again.

Michael used to help Mama to the bathroom when all he had to do was stand outside the door and wait on her to finish her business so he could lead her back to bed. That stopped when she required help inside. I had to put her in diapers. It broke my heart, but Mama never seemed to notice.

I unlocked the door without making a sound, thanks to years of practice. Daddy, stretched out in the recliner, didn't even notice when I squeezed between his chair and the metal buffet to get through and go to my room.

I changed into my pajamas in the dark and crawled into bed, wondering if it was spooky or comforting to sleep under a canopy. Rather than let it play on my mind and keep me awake all night, I pulled the covers up over my head and then poked them up in the center with one foot. I stayed that way until my leg went to sleep, just to get the feel of having cloth overhead. It wasn't spooky or comforting, but my tingling leg might have taken away from the true affect.

Chapter 6

David pounded my bedroom door with his fist, trying to punch a new hole in it from the sound of things. "Get up, Sleeping Beauty, your mother wants you."

My mother needed me – maybe. I doubted she wanted me, and knew she didn't ask for me. She didn't call anyone by name any more, and she hadn't asked for anything specifically in years. She moaned and hollered, nonsense mostly.

When she formed real words or sentences, it seemed accidental since they weren't ever fitting to the situation. I asked what she wanted for dinner one night and she screamed out something about the dust mop. I stopped asking for her input after that. She only wanted to holler; she didn't want anything particular and she didn't want me. David was shirking his responsibility.

I pulled my arm out from under the pillow and pushed the curtain aside to look at the clock on the windowsill. The set-up still disappointed me. I wanted to use the curtains like a headboard, but when I turned the bed in that position there wasn't enough room left to open the door. Placing the bed long ways under the window ruined the whole idea, but at least I had the matching comforter and curtains I had always wanted – one Cinderella dream accomplished – and I could see the clock without getting up for my glasses.

I was sitting on the last bus, eight blocks from home, with my first GWS paycheck in my purse when the idea hit me. I got off the bus at the next stop, turned around and got on another one going right back where I came from, and went straight to K-mart. I set out with just the comforter and curtains in mind, but found a packaged set with matching sheets, a dust ruffle, and a pillow sham and bought the whole thing.

At one point, I had a throw rug and decorator pillow in my cart. I counseled myself about greed all the way through the store and up until I was next in line at the cash register, and ended up getting out of line to put them back on the shelf. Mama may not have said anything for real at that time, but her old words came back in my mind often enough. "Clarice, be grateful you get what you need. Asking for anything more is downright greedy."

Ten o'clock. I hadn't slept that late since I was a kid and Daddy still had his job at the meat packing company and we could depend on a little quiet during the day. You would have thought he got rid of all his meanness knocking animals in the head with a hammer all day, but he didn't. He saved plenty for when he came home.

Back then, Mama got up early to make his breakfast and see him off to work. During summer break and on school holidays she left David and Michael and me to sleep in, probably, I realized much later, to get a little peace from us. Still, it felt like a good thing.

After Daddy left for work, Mama went about cleaning the trailer as quiet as a mouse but with walls that thin I heard the kitchen chairs scoot across the linoleum, and the broom scrape under the table. And shortly after the seat clicked against the tank, I'd hear the scratch of the toilet bowl brush. Sometimes she hummed or sang a song while she worked. She never did that when we were up so I'd stay in bed as long as I could stand it just to hear her sing. When I was little, I thought she was good enough to make records. Later, I didn't know if that was just a little girl's dream or the truth and by then she had stopped singing at all.

When the aroma of the lemon Pledge she used to shine the single end table that had once been her grandmother's made its way under my door, I smiled. I knew she was loading that table up with three layers of polish to protect it in case Daddy or the boys set a wet glass or beer bottle on it when she wasn't looking. A glass on the end table was the only thing that set Mama off, and probably the only thing that didn't set Daddy off. That's how far apart they were in their thinking.

Weekends were a different story – then and now. Whether anyone got to sleep in – or sleep at all, really – depended entirely on how and where Daddy did his drinking. If we were lucky, he went to one of his favorite bars or to a poker party at a friend's house. Once he got out, we could depend on him to stay out most of the night, unless he got in a fight, in which case he came back home to drink. The fight nights were the worst because he started out in a bad mood and it got progressively worse the more he drank. Nobody got any sleep until he passed out. Sometimes that took well into the next day.

Once in a while, he came in from work packing a case of beer and proclaimed it *family night*. Every time, David said he wanted to be an orphan. Behind Daddy's back, Mama told me family night really meant Daddy didn't pay his tab so they cut him off at the bar.

Family nights started out better than bar nights because he was in a good mood until after the first few drinks, but those nights usually ended worse. It was family night the first time David carted the recliner out front.

Before we finished chewing the last bites of our food, Daddy started in yelling at Mama for her to hurry and clear the mess out of the kitchen so we could have the table clear for Monopoly. Michael stood on a chair to carefully pull the taped up game box down from its place on top of the kitchen cabinet.

Everyone had to play, whether we wanted to or not. Mama tried to find a thousand and one excuses every time why she couldn't play – she needed to get the clothes together for the Laundromat in the morning; she wanted to bake a cake, she had a headache – but he never let her off the hook. Family included everyone.

Mama went for the TV tray and set it up next to the kitchen table for Daddy to use as the bank, and took her seat beside me. She was the thimble and I was the shoe.

Daddy didn't trust anyone else to be banker. He counted the starter money out and delivered it with the same explanation every time. "One of you yahoos lost half of the money. Until I get an apology, nobody gets their full count. Got that?" David reminded him once that he was the one who threw the money out the door in the snow, and Daddy took back an extra fifty from David for lying. He shorted Mama out of principle because she raised us wrong, leaving him the only one who got the full amount.

It really didn't matter if we got our money or not, or that half of the money was missing or all of the property cards had been taped back together after he tore them up, or that there were only four houses and no hotels left. We all knew the game would end long before the hotel stage, with Daddy pitching a fit about something that didn't really happen anywhere except in his imagination, and declaring himself winner.

I caught on real early that David pissed Daddy off on purpose, and sooner each time we played, just to get it over with.

While Michael gathered the remnants of the game, and taped anything that needed to be taped, Mama folded the TV tray back down and stuck it behind the couch. David and I sat on the couch and waited for everyone else to join us for the second event – family television.

Daddy sat in his recliner and yelled out for somebody to switch the channel so often we got dizzy. We didn't have a remote control like everybody else, because he wouldn't give up the old console TV and old console TVs didn't come with remote controls. He never left it on any program for more than ten seconds and he never asked what anyone else wanted to watch. We didn't make suggestions.

David seldom made it through an hour of television without starting trouble, either. He complained that he was bored, or accused Michael of hogging more than his share of the couch. And then he let out exaggerated sighs that got on everyone's nerves, especially Daddy's.

The rest of us gave David dirty looks because all his complaining was going to do was get us a lecture about the value of family time. "Some kids don't have a father that wants to spend time with them," he'd say, shaking a finger at us. "Hell, some kids don't have a father. You should count your blessings."

The lecture lasted approximately six beers, unless David was in what Mama called rare form. In rare form, David was so obnoxious that even Daddy couldn't battle with him, so he'd run through the case of beer in no time. If he was still conscious when the beer ran out, he went to Truman's trailer down the block and drank up his beer. Either way, passed out or gone to Truman's, we could finally go to bed.

If David failed to work up a rare form, Daddy drank slow and went from one lecture right into the next. Sometimes we sat there all night listening and never got any sleep.

David pounded on the door again. "Did you hear me in there?"

I opened the door and walked past him to the bathroom, thinking how unbelievable it was that I had gone from heaven to hell in less than twenty-four hours. One minute I was sitting on the side of a pool with my feet dipped in and less than a day later I was filling a plastic bucket with warm water to wash my Mama up with.

I tucked a towel and washcloth under my arm and headed for her room. I always knew, or at least hoped, that one day I'd crawl out of bed to change diapers. I just thought I'd be the mama, not the other way around.

I washed her up and changed her into a clean gown, trying to bring a little cheer as I worked. "How are you feeling this morning, Mama? You look rested. I think that lava lamp kept you good company last night."

So much wasted breath. She responded in grunts, spoken without eye contact or recognition. But I had to try, since the doctor couldn't say for sure if she understood or not. I didn't want her to think I gave up.

"I'm sorry I left you with the boys yesterday. I went to a really nice party at my new friend Rena's house. Well, it isn't her house any more. She has her own apartment now. Her parents still live there. Mama, can you hear me?" She gave no indication that she could, so I said I'd be back in a little while with her breakfast.

I put bread in the toaster and turned to David, sitting at the table reading yesterday's paper because he was too lazy to walk to the corner for the new edition. The person who made up the saying *a day late and a dollar short* must have had David in mind.

"Would it have hurt you to fix her something to eat?" I asked.

"You dumped her on me all day yesterday. It's your turn, Cinderella. Me and Michael take care of her Monday through Friday. Weekends are yours, remember?"

I reminded him that I fed her breakfast and dinner every day and left her lunch prepared for them when I had to work. Someone in the family had to work.

He didn't hear me right. Not with any sense in his listening. His answer was, "Bitch, bitch, bitch, Clarice. I'm sick of your whining."

"I'm sick of you sitting on your butt while I pay the bills and do all the work," I said. "One of these days I'm going to find a life of my own and leave you guys to fend for yourselves. You'll be sorry."

David laughed. "Yeah, right, Cinderella, your prince charming is pulling in the trailer court as we speak."

"I'm going to Emily's house after I feed Mama. You'll have to take care of her today." I put Mama's breakfast on a tray and walked out before he could answer.

I took a gamble that one of them would watch over her while I was gone.

~~~

I sat between the stop sign and the wooden placard that warned people they were entering the twilight zone. *Shady Acres Trailer Park* made about as much sense as Mama's blabbering. How could there be shade without trees or tall buildings? The word *acres* conjures up expectations sure to be disappointed by blacktop ribbons running through dirt patches sprinkled with rocks.

While I waited my turn to pull out on Highway 24, I decided there was another way to look at the sign. I was exiting the twilight zone and entering shady acres. The trees and acres lived on the other side; I had seen them the day before.

Excitement swelled again, this time building more subtly than before. I took time to focus on the memories – the house that looked like a museum, tables full of food and drinks, big tents and too many bathrooms, and people who didn't look at me like they knew I lived in Shady Acres Trailer Park off Highway 24. It was a new day and the Escort hadn't turned into a pumpkin. I let go of the urge to pinch myself to see if I was dreaming and just let myself soak up the good feelings like a sponge.

Things looked brighter and more detailed. I saw individual leaves on trees and blades of grass instead of patches of green, and real life faces inside the cars that passed me. When I got in town, I smiled and nodded my head at a man in a Lexus. He had a wide nose and a moustache – I looked close enough to know that because I looked him straight in the eye without even considering if he was offended by my Escort. He smiled back at me.

It was too nice a day to waste it sitting inside, especially in Emily's second story apartment where her dad would have the windows shut to keep out the street noise. In no time, it would be sweltering so I didn't even want to go there. I wanted to go to some real shady acres to talk, maybe the waterfront park. I wished Emily had a phone so I could call and tell her to be ready.

Emily tried to get phone service for her family shortly after she went full time at the bank, but the landlord wouldn't give his consent to the phone company for the lines to be run into his property. Their downstairs neighbor let Emily's family use her mobile phone for emergencies, but this wasn't an emergency.

Another great idea popped in my head. I'd take Emily to shop for a cell phone. We could talk about the party on the way to the mall.

I sat in front of the house blowing the horn until Emily came down and got in the car.

"Are they still having church at St. Leo's?" she asked. "It's kind of late."

"I didn't even go there first," I explained. "I had a great idea. Go get your purse so we can go shopping."

"I can't spend any money, Clarice. What are you up to?"

Emily didn't need a Cinderella account. Her teeth were straight, and she had 20/20 vision, straight hair, and some meat on her bones. She never seemed to notice, which was good for not being conceited but I told her, at least once a week, to thank her lucky stars for all that good luck. She didn't have to be conceited in order to appreciate what she got.

Emily tucked away every cent she could for a car, and she was a lot closer to her goal than I was to mine. In fact, she had enough put back to buy a junker already, but she was holding out for another five hundred, at least. Her parents helped her out by not making her pay room and board, and by actually paying their own bills, unlike someone I knew.

"How much were you willing to pay for the telephone if Mr. Brown would have signed for it? Can you still afford that much? I thought we could check out those cell phone deals where two people share an account. I don't need many minutes. I'd just like to have the phone around if I break down or something. We could get the cheapest plan if you want."

I expected Emily to be excited, but she sat there chewing on her lip while she mulled it over for what seemed like forever and a day.

"What's the deal here, Clarice? You spent one day at a hoity-toity party and now you think you need a cell phone? What's next, a Mercedes?"

"That party has nothing to do with this. I mainly wanted you to have a phone." She hurt my feelings a little with that comment about hoity-toity because she didn't even know Rena. "I thought I could help you keep the cost down if we do it this way."

I drove around the block so I wouldn't hold up traffic while Emily went upstairs to get her purse, and thought about what she had said. I decided against mentioning the party again to Emily unless she specifically asked me a question.

"We don't have to look at cell phones," I told her when we pulled away. "We can go to the waterfront and feed the ducks if you'd rather."

Emily said she guessed it wouldn't hurt to check the phones out. But she was wrong. Neither of us had enough credit to qualify for a regular account. One company offered us a pre-paid account, but we would have had to buy two phones, at ninety-eight dollars apiece, and our rates would have been much higher than the regular account rates unless we just packed the things around and never used them.

"I don't understand," I said. Actually, I did understand, but I wanted to question the point without making the salesclerk mad. "If we're pre-paid, you know you get your money from us. Why ask more of us than of the people who might skip out and not pay?"

"It's company policy," the unfriendly clerk said.

Emily laughed. "I guess that means he doesn't understand either."

I didn't laugh with her. "This makes me mad, Emily. I want an explanation. Because neither of us makes a habit of buying things we can't afford, we don't have credit. And because we don't have credit, they don't want our business."

"I think they're afraid we won't pay the bill," Emily explained.

"Look at the deal. If we sign up, we pay them for a month of service in advance, and every month when we make our payment, we would actually be paying for the next month. If we didn't make the payment, they'd cut us off. Everyone is pre-paid, really. So they can't lose. Credit isn't necessary in the first place. As if that isn't a smack in the face already, he tries to sell us a deal where we can get half as much for twice the cost."

I glared at the salesclerk, waiting for an explanation that I never got. I had half a mind to stand there the rest of the day and hold up his line.

"Do I look like some kind of idiot?" I asked. "No, wait. Don't answer that. I guess I do, since my brothers have told me that nearly every day of my life." I wiped the corners of my mouth with the butt of my hand because I was too excited to talk slow and swallow often. "I'm not as stupid as I look, and you can bet that one day, when I'm in a better position, I won't be back here to open an account."

I stormed out of the store with Emily trailing a step behind.

"What's gotten into you, Clarice? I've never seen you act like this."

I got in the car fast because I didn't want everyone in the Bittersweet Shopping Alcove to see how upset I was. I pulled my glasses off to wipe a stream of tears on the hem of my shirt and tried to explain.

"I'm tired of being treated like dirt just because I'm poor."

Emily nodded. "Did somebody insult you at that party?"

"No!" I slipped my glasses back on and grasped the steering wheel until the knuckles on both hands went white. "This isn't about the party. Those people were very nice to me. For once, I felt like I belonged somewhere. This is about the rest of my life, before and after the party."

"Clarice, nothing's ever going to change. Just ignore the ugly people you meet and hang on to the nice ones. That's all you can do. Now, start driving and get your mind off this. Let's go feed the ducks."

I listened to Emily recount her week while we fed the mallards that braved a walk up the grassy hill to eat from our hands. "We had a big meeting on Wednesday and they announced a couple of new employee benefits. We only get to choose one. I'm thinking about going for the tuition reimbursement. My boss said I could probably work my way up to head teller if I'm in school, and maybe even to manager when I finish."

That pulled me momentarily out of the fog the cell phone clerk had cast over me. "That's great news, Em. When are you going to start?"

"When I get my car. I can't ride the bus to and from work, and then again to school and keep up with a job and schoolwork. As soon as I get a car, I'll start taking classes."

I drove Emily back to Paine Avenue, half-listening to her explain what she had retained from the 401K presentation at that same meeting. It looked like Emily had a chance to make a real life for herself. I had to help her get there.

"I'm not going to park, Em, I need to get back home to Mama. Will you do me a favor?"

"Sure. What do you need?"

"I want you to go ahead and pick up an application for school. I'll drive you until you get your car."

Chapter 7

After twelve hours of dead-to-the-world sleep, I skipped the snooze button and made it to work on time – in matching clothes and shoes. Clarice sat her coffee mug down on the counter and came over to place the back of her hand on my forehead.

"I think you must be coming down with something, Girlfriend. You're five whole minutes early."

"Smart-Alek," I teased, pushing her hand away. "Don't get your hopes up. This freak accident occurred only because I fell asleep at five o'clock last night and slept straight through. I can almost promise it will never happen again."

Clarice watched me put my purse in the bottom drawer of the empty file cabinet by the window, fill my stained mug with coffee, remove the closed sign from my window, and climb onto my stool before asking, ""Now, doesn't it feel good when you aren't rushed? I love coming in here early so I can take my time and have a few minutes to relax before customers start lining up."

I thought about the question before the editorial and answered it honestly. "I actually think I enjoy chaos, Clarice. I guess that's a negative reflection on my boring life, isn't it? The only excitement I get is in rushing to work."

"Maybe you're making up for your time in the museum." Her voice softened. "Thanks for inviting me to the barbecue, Rena. I think it's probably the most fun I've ever had." She looked embarrassed, probably wishing she hadn't said the last part.

"Thank you for coming, Clarice. I enjoyed getting to know you away from work. And, honestly, I would have been bored to tears if you weren't there. Probably would have left much earlier."

I hoped I had given back enough to make her feel like we were equally vulnerable, so she would return to her fun personality. The soft-spoken, timid side of her made me uneasy.

With a somber expression, she left an uncomfortably long silence before she spoke again. "One of these days I'll reciprocate. Is that the right word? Maybe the McDaniels family will have another bring-a-dish-keg party and I can invite you."

I detected a hint of elevation in her voice and tried to draw her further away from the somber mood. "That sounds like fun. Closer to my kind of party than Mother's was."

"Baked beans are already spoken for, so you'll have to think what else you want to bring."

"Paper plates," I offered. "Do your guests a favor and assign me to something I can't mess up." It felt like we were back on track.

"If it will make you feel more at home, I'll ask my brother to park your car."

I waited for her to snort or slurp, anything to assure me that she was kidding, but a customer walked up to her window. She transformed immediately into super-rep.

She mentioned a brother. A glimpse into her personal life felt like progress.

Clarice listened patiently to her customer's run down of unexpected expenses in the last month. The battery died in the car; her son lost a tennis shoe in the locker room at school and she had to buy a new pair; the air-conditioner went out; and her daughter was invited to a birthday party and couldn't go without a gift. All in one month. The woman actually stood in front of Clarice's window and sobbed like a child who had lost her favorite toy. It would take forever to catch up with everything but she promised the water bill would be the next bill she paid just please don't shut her off.

"Can you pay anything on your balance?" Clarice asked the question in a soft, understanding voice.

"Only about thirty dollars," the woman answered. "That's half. Can you accept half?"

Clarice instructed the customer to wait on the bench in the lobby. "I have to get permission from my supervisor. I'll come get you after I talk to him."

"I learn something new every day," I said, after the customer was out of hearing range. "Who are we supposed to talk to about partial payments?"

"I usually contact my guardian angel first, and God second," she said. "Rena, GWS won't accept partial payments. The birthday party got to me. I have an idea."

I couldn't believe my ears. Surely, the perfect Clarice McDaniels wasn't thinking of something dishonest, like deleting her balance, or accidentally removing this woman's address from the shut-off list.

I discovered a new talent, amazed at how quickly those illegal acts came to mind. Knowing Clarice, she had a much better idea. I tried, but couldn't think of another way to keep the lady's service without a payment.

"What are you going to do?"

Before I finished the question, I noticed Clarice was on her feet with her purse over her shoulder. Her closed sign was already up.

"Will you cover for me? I'll be back in five minutes. If anybody asks, I'm in the bathroom."

I said sure, especially curious now that I knew her plan required leaving her desk, with her purse. I had a fleeting vision of Clarice standing in front of Jordan Hall, Director of the Billing Department, holding a gun to his head while she demanded that he accept the partial payment her customer offered – or else.

"Clarice, you aren't thinking of doing anything crazy are you?"

"It's crazy enough, but not illegal or dangerous or anything like that. I'm going to the automatic teller machine."

I tried to stop her. "You're here to collect money from customers, not give it to them. You can't do this."

Suddenly, many of the things I questioned before made perfect sense - the number of customers who made payments in person, the brownies and flowers. I understood why they were so disappointed when they ended up in my line instead of Clarice's.

"I can," she said, "and I will. It's only thirty dollars. Just cover for me. I'll hurry."

I sighed. "Sit down. I have thirty dollars in my purse I can lend you until lunchtime. You can stop at the ATM and pay me back then."

This idea was crazy enough. She didn't need to make it worse by taking the chance that anyone in management might catch her out of the building while she was on the clock.

"Thanks, Rena. I'll pay you back at lunch, I promise.

Clarice called her customer back to the window. "How soon can you pay the balance? My boss says we won't shut you off if you promise to come back within two weeks and pay the balance."

The lady promised.

"You need to come to my window," Clarice warned, "because I'll have the paperwork here. Please don't let me down. If you don't come back, GWS will take this amount out of my check and I won't be able to buy my mother's heart medicine."

"I promise. I'll be here next Friday. You can count on me. Thank you so much." With tears threatening to spill from her tired eyes, the customer squeezed Clarice's hand and said. "Bless you dear."

We stopped at the ATM on the way to Grant's Cafeteria and Clarice paid me back.

"Do you really have to buy your mother's heart medicine?" I asked.

Clarice looked away and spoke quickly. "That was a white lie. I consider it sort of like an insurance policy. Only a snake would take a chance on my mother's heart medicine, and I didn't think that lady was a snake. Not when she said she had to buy the birthday present."

She didn't offer any more information about her mother, other than that she didn't really have to buy her medicine. I thought I'd try for something else. "Do you really have a brother?"

"That part was true. I have two brothers. Rena, please don't tell anyone I paid this lady's water bill. Ann would shit a brick over this."

Obviously she wasn't going to discuss her family. I said I wouldn't tell anyone what she had done, and delivered a mini-lecture about being too generous for her own good. She listened with a stonewall expression and I knew I was wasting my breath.

I really wanted to ask her why the birthday present meant so much to her, but resisted and let her choose a topic instead. She talked about the party. "Your mother looks like she could be your sister. She's very pretty."

I agreed. My mother looked great for her age. "Mother was always attractive, but she owes a good deal of her preservation to Larry. He lifted the eyes and tucked the tummy for her."

Clarice looked disappointed, but let me know quickly that it wasn't Mother who generated that reaction. "Rena, why are you so hard on your mother? There's nothing wrong with wanting to lift and tuck a few things. If it makes her happy, why do you care? Don't you want her to be happy?"

The heat in my face was bound to be visible. I was shocked that Clarice had so openly criticized me, although she had done it in the kindest way possible – by forcing me to question myself.

But that wasn't the worst feeling I possessed at the moment. What had I done? Had I assumed that Clarice would be offended by mother's offers when, in fact, she would have been thrilled with them? What if I had rejected her dreams because I thought I knew something about her that I didn't know at all?

I wanted to tell her about Mother's phone call, then throw myself at her feet and beg forgiveness. An even mix of sorrow, embarrassment, and shame robbed me of my appetite. I left a full plate of fish and broccoli sitting on the table at Grant's Cafeteria while I tried to sift through my feelings.

"Clarice, everything is so complex with my mother. I'm an only child because she had a hard time losing the weight after I was born. I wished for a brother or sister to share secrets and good times with, and someone to have tea parties with in the lonely playhouse that sat at the back of the yard so it wouldn't detract from the landscaping around the pool. I missed out on things that were important to me so she could have what she wanted more – a flat stomach.

"Then she started with the implants and tucks and sucks here and there because she thought it was important to stay attractive for her profession. Tell me, Clarice, how disappointing is that?"

She played with her food, swirling mashed potatoes around on her plate, seeming to have lost her appetite, too. Finally, she shrugged and spoke without taking her eyes off the potatoes. "I guess it is important to look nice if you're a lawyer."

"Looking nice includes being clean and appropriately dressed. Do you honestly think the judge and jury decide cases based on which attorney has the biggest boobs, the flattest stomach, or the fewest lines around their eyes? If so, God help us all, because the legal system sucks worse than I thought."

Clarice giggled. "Girlfriend, you're funny when you get all worked up like this. But I see were you're coming from."

I went to bed early that night, planning to recover the work ethics I left behind me in Dr. Crane's office. So what if I didn't get hired for the job I wanted; I still owed it to the company to show up on time. Clarice's guilt trip worked, even if that wasn't what she had in mind.

The birthday party won out over sleep. I couldn't stop thinking how strange it was that the woman's birthday party gift weighed in over the broken air-conditioner and dead battery, even for a softy like Clarice. Not for the longest time.

The phantom pain came in the middle of the night. Clarice must have known a Sissy Eickle.

Chapter 8

Dad waited until he was in his car on the way to the hospital to return my call. I had called him early, while he was still at home, but I called on his cell phone. He knew the drill; using his cell during off hours instead of the house phone meant I didn't want Mother to know I was calling.

I answered on the first ring. "I'm okay, Dad, and I don't need money."

That got me a deep belly laugh, followed by questions in a gruff tone that I knew was fake. "Then what are you doing up this early? Don't you know, only surgeons, paperboys, and daughters who are doing things their fathers don't want to know about are out of bed before six?"

I snapped my head around to look at the clock on my nightstand, so afraid it had earned a position on the undependable side with my old boyfriends.

"It's six-thirty, Dad. Are you sure *you're* okay?"

"Rena, you answered your phone playfully instead of taking my head off, so I know you've been awake for more than thirty minutes. If you're trying to be coy, or mysterious, you need to develop your strategy a little better."

"Okay, you got me. But I wasn't trying to be either of those." I stalled, because now that he was on the phone I didn't know exactly what I wanted to ask him.

"I also know you didn't wake up this early to call because you miss me. I know you much better than that, Rena. What's up?"

"Dad, do you remember Sissy Eickle, the little girl who crashed my eighth birthday party?"

"Hold on," he warned. "There's a tunnel ahead."

While I waited for his cell phone to pick up the signal again, it dawned on me that I had never considered how difficult my father's life had been. He got up this early every day, often after a middle of the night emergency phone call or two, and was usually scrubbed and ready to hold someone's brain or spinal cord in his hand by seven. No wonder I was expected to keep things quiet at home in the evenings. He deserved his rest.

His voice came back, surrounded by crackling interference. "I wouldn't have remembered the child's name if you hadn't stated it, but I do remember your mother's reaction when the girl showed up at the party without an invitation. Charlotte was so afraid you would catch head lice from her. There was quite an epidemic that year, totally unresponsive to over-the-counter remedies.

"You had such a mess of hair, and she was in the middle of some huge trial that had her on pins and needles for months. I can't believe I'm remembering all of this." He paused, and I could picture the creases on his brow as he tried to figure out why he remembered. "I think that was around the time Charlotte's mother was diagnosed with that colon problem, too. What a time that was. Why are you awake at this hour asking me about Sissy? Did something happen to her?"

"It's a long story, Dad. Can we talk about it later?"

He reminded me that I had initiated this early morning communication and now I was putting him off.

"I'm not trying to put you off," I explained. "I'm asking for an appointment so we can sit down and discuss this. When can I see you?"

"Let me transfer you to my receptionist and see what she has available," he teased. "It's usually a two week wait, and you'll need a referral from your primary physician if you expect your insurance to cover my fee."

"Ha ha ha," I said, without humor. "You're pushing your luck with this early morning comedy routine already."

We made a date for lunch. He told me to choose a place and wait for him in front of GWS at eleven. If I wanted to bring Clarice, she was welcome to join us, his treat.

In addition to matching clothes and shoes, I even had time left to apply a touch of mascara and lipstick and still beat Clarice in to work by ten minutes. She grabbed her chest when she saw me. "Girlfriend, are you trying to give me a heart attack or something coming in this early? You promised yesterday was an accident that wouldn't happen again. And look at you! She walked a circle around me, zeroing in on my face. "You look really pretty with make-up."

A lump formed in my throat, making my thank you squeak out as a whisper. I cleared my throat and tried again.

"Thank you, Clarice. That one didn't sound generic and I honestly appreciate it."

She tossed her head back and rolled her eyes. This time I watched as she locked her purse in the empty file cabinet and poured a cup of coffee. She did look peaceful, and I hoped I hadn't intruded on the solitude she looked forward to in the mornings.

When she came back to open her window, I told her I was having lunch with Dad, so she'd have plenty of time to make other plans if she wanted, feeling another twinge of guilt because I knew she would have liked to join us. But I needed this time alone with him to sort out my confusion about her.

"I'll probably work through lunch and get some overtime," she decided. "Ann used to let me do that a lot before you came. Then she didn't have to send her secretary over."

I watched Clarice work for a few minutes, searching for something in her demeanor or personality – some telltale or psychic hint that she was the least bit dissatisfied with her appearance. I found nothing. Clarice portrayed confidence and dignity. Even her worn clothes transmitted pride. I knew a tremendous amount of maintenance and creativity went into keeping them attractive and stylish. I noticed the new set of buttons on the old, rose-colored blouse, and the addition of a scarf around the fraying neckline of her green dress. The same pair of navy slacks looked completely different with the white ruffle blouse tucked in and belted on Monday, than they looked on Friday with the jersey knit top worn over the waistband.

"Okay Girlfriend, if you keep staring like that I'll have to charge you for a private viewing."

"I was just thinking." I started but wasn't sure how to proceed.

She slurped her coffee. "Thinking is a good thing, Rena. Keep doing it, just look somewhere else while you do. You're giving me a big head staring at me that way."

"Clarice, do you really think my make-up looks okay? I never got into primping much, so I don't really know much about how to apply cosmetics or style my hair. Because I don't keep up with the latest styles, I only used a little mascara and lipstick. I've had it so long it's probably contaminated. The only manicure I've ever had was the one Mother arranged before my senior prom. Guess I'm feeling a little self-conscious."

"That's right," she remembered. "You didn't do the sleepovers. That's where most girls experiment with those things. I never was much for sleepovers either, but I practiced a lot on my friend Emily's hair. For a while, I thought I wanted to be a cosmetologist. I'm good with hair, but not so much with make-up or nails."

I tried to sound spontaneous and excited. "Let's go have a make-over, Clarice. It might be fun if we do it together."

The sour look on her face when she turned around made me immediately sorry I had made the suggestion. "Do you mean like those things on the Oprah Show or something? No offense, Rena, but I don't think so. You'll have to do that without me."

Relieved, I explained that Oprah wasn't what I had in mind I didn't think she was even still on television. "I was thinking more in the line of going to the cosmetic counter in a department store."

Her expression didn't change. She still looked like she had been sucking lemons. "And be on display for all the other customers to gawk at? Not me."

"Better yet," I tried again, "maybe we can invite an Avon or Mary Kay representative to come in for a private make-over. We can do it at my apartment."

She agreed to think about that one.

"Even if you decide against the make-over," I asked, "will you still think about coming over to help me learn to do something with my hair?"

She played with one of her gelled spikes and said maybe.

I chose an Italian restaurant, not because Dad or I were either one particularly crazy about Italian, but because it was one of the nicer places located near GWS. He thanked me for making his head itch all morning and I said no problem. "I couldn't stop thinking about lice," he explained. "Are you ready to tell me what this is all about?"

"It's not really about lice or about Sissy," I confessed. "It's about Clarice. Well, maybe it's about me, and then again it could be about Mother, or all of us. I'm so confused, Dad."

"It sounds that way. Your mother asked me something about Clarice the other night."

I rolled my eyes. "Did she try to solicit a free craniotomy for her? Dad, I was so upset with Mother for trying to change everything about Clarice, and for calling other people to ask for charity in Clarice's name. But now

69

I'm afraid I might have been thinking more of myself than of Clarice."

"How so?" he asked.

"You know how I get with Mother. I let everything she says rub me the wrong way. When she said the only reason I invited Clarice to the party was to introduce her to people who could help her, I became too defensive to think about her suggestions rationally."

"Why did you invite her?"

Come on, not him too. Surely he hadn't let Mother convince him that I wanted charity for my *poor little friend.*

"Because I like her, and because I thought everyone else might see in her what I see – a very nice, fun person – not a project. I asked her because I thought I'd have a better time with her there. I thought she had something to give to your guests, not the other way around. If I were planning a party, I'd want people like her to show up."

He reached across the table to pat my hand, and we ate our salads without speaking another word. When the entrees arrived, we talked about anything but Clarice and my motives for inviting her to the party.

The waitress cleared our plates from the table and said she'd be right back with the check and I was disappointed because Dad still hadn't offered any advice. When he finally returned to the topic, he still didn't. "Rena, what does any of this have to do with Sissy?"

I shrugged my shoulders. "I don't know. But it's all connected somehow. You're supposed to know about brains."

"Not that way. I sure can't read your mind." He paid the waitress and stood to leave and didn't return to the subject until we were in the GWS parking lot and I was getting out of his car. "Let me know when you get it all figured out."

Clarice was handing her customer a receipt for his late payment when I returned. When he walked away, I handed her two breadsticks wrapped in a paper napkin. "They brought a whole basket and we couldn't eat them all. Dad can't stand to see anything go to waste and I'm stuffed, so you're stuck with these."

She thanked me and took a bite. I took the next three customers so she wouldn't have to talk with her mouth full. During a slow period later in the afternoon, she asked what I wanted to do with my hair.

"I'm open to suggestions," I told her. "I'm ready for a change, but not sure what I want or need."

"We'll come up with something," she promised. "Let me think on it a day or two."

I should have warned her then that I didn't' like to spend much time on my hair and I was allergic to most sprays and gels. She had probably figured the first part out without me telling her.

~~~

The glamour and primping phase lost its opportunity to seize me during the preteen stage where it typically caught most girls. I was vulnerable on one day, when Jen's older sister allowed us to practice with her cosmetics.

We tried out different colors and techniques all afternoon, and I finally went home wearing a thick black line across my eyelid that extended almost far enough to meet the outside edge of my eyebrow. Thinking I was possibly the most beautiful twelve-year-old girl anyone had ever seen, I rushed up to have my parents confirm that for me. The look on my Mother's face when she saw me dispelled that fantasy very quickly.

"Everyone else in my class wears make-up," did nothing to win her over. She wasn't everyone else's mother and I wasn't going to run around looking like some street corner hooker or a freak out of a music video - not as long as I was her daughter. I wondered if that position was optional, and if so, how did I go about resigning and finding a mother who appreciated my beauty. She would allow me to wear lip-gloss after my next birthday. End of discussion.

71

I told my friends I liked my sleep too much to get up earlier just so I could spend an hour in front of the mirror before I came to school. They shrugged me off as a hopeless case but left me alone about my hair and lack of make-up.

When mother finally decided I was old enough to wear make-up, I couldn't think of any logical reason to explain why I had changed my mind about sleep, so I stuck with the story. By then, painted faces and sprayed hair had lost their appeal anyway. Before long, my sleep did mean that much to me – on the waking up end at least.

Ironically, when I decided I didn't want to invest my time or money in cosmetics, hair care, clothes, or plastic surgery, Mother developed an obsession with changing me into exactly what she had worked so diligently to discourage before. We reversed positions. She tried to force me to (her words) *take pride* in my appearance, insinuating that it would take all of those things to make me attractive, and maybe when I worked at it, I could attract *a keeper.*

The more she pushed, the harder I resisted anything concerning glamour, or even appearance. Consequently, I didn't know how to arrange a private makeover. Mother surely knew, but I couldn't ask her without admitting that I was considering the legitimacy of her concern for Clarice, or giving her false hope that I might one day give up my wash-and-wear appearance.

Maybe the Avon representative who left catalogues at my door for over a year would forget that I tossed them all in the trash unopened and drop another out there. Or, I might run into someone like Lori Zeller's pinched-faced, obese mother, who unloaded her cosmetics to groups of women gathered in someone's home under the guise of a party.

Lori convinced our dorm monitor to set up folding tables in the lobby one Sunday afternoon so her mother could bring in cases of cosmetics and convert everyone in our building into super-model level beauties. The profits from her sales would go toward repairing the damage Lori had caused to my car.

I agreed to be there as a spectator, but refused to participate in the demonstration. Halfway through, I congratulated myself on that decision. Later, I thought about running over to the psychology department to see if anyone was interested in studying the masochistic relevance of voluntary criticism of bone structure, skin tone, and oily spots.

The willing victims secured their hair away from their faces with plastic headbands and used the cleansing formulas Lori's mother squeezed into their palms to remove the improper cosmetics they had worn to the party. They looked like ghosts to me because I was so used to seeing them a different color than they actually were; and they looked like they had seen ghosts when they saw each other's bare faces. The whole thing was positively frightening.

Lori's mother used their discarded cotton balls to point out the disgusting impurities most of them had collected in their pores. Would any of them ever be able to look each other in the eye again without remembering how much dirt the other produced on her cotton ball? Four years later, my stomach still turned when I thought about some of them.

After a thorough cleansing and moisturizing, their faces were ready for Lori's mother to scrutinize them for structural defects. Larry Forbes could have retired on the flat chests and skeletal defects in the room. One face was too wide through the brow area and another forehead was too long. There were pointed chins, square chins, long noses, eyes set too far apart and others too close together, and not a perfect set of lips in the crowd.

The girls leaned in toward their plastic mirrors to study their imperfections, quieter than I had ever seen them as a group. I was stunned, to think that a group of girls not yet old enough to order an alcoholic beverage were already in desperate need of so much help.

Lori buzzed around the table clearing their filthy cotton balls and tissues away and replaced them with pallets and disposable brushes. Her mother restored hope. She hoisted the cases on the table and unlatched the covers, promising she had something in there that would cure or mask every one of their imperfections. She pulled out tubes and bottles and trays of powders and ran around the room dropping samples on their pallets.

They stayed for hours, while Lori's mother showed each of them how to shade, shadow and shape their disgusting, misshapen faces into painted perfection. No one appeared to notice that Lori's mother was wearing at least an ounce of every magic potion she demonstrated on her own face, and her eyes were still too close together, her nose too thin, and her mouth resembled a cheerio.

I wasn't sure I wanted to put myself, or Clarice, through that. What was I thinking when I made the suggestion? I must have been thinking the same insulting thoughts about Clarice that I was upset with my mother for expressing.

Oh God! I was turning into my mother – far before the expected age for that transformation.

I panicked over the dilemma I had put myself in. If Clarice decided to go along with my makeover suggestion, I had no way to renege without hurting her feelings and making a fool of myself. I deserved worse than the anguish of having the bone structure of my face analyzed.

I decided I would follow Clarice's lead. With any luck, she would realize it was rude of me to suggest the makeover, and even ruder to assume that I would prefer that it take place at my apartment instead of her home, and tactfully decline my misguided, selfish invitation. If not, I would deliver the most exciting makeover a girl could ask for. The ball was in her court, and I sure hoped she missed it.

Chapter 9

My idea of a big Friday night out was for Daddy and the boys to be out so I could have some peace at home. For some reason, Mama's hollering didn't wear on my serenity like theirs did and that reason was probably that her hollering was no threat to anybody. She wasn't aiming to hurt feelings and wasn't likely going to break furniture or rip up Monopoly cards.

Daddy had given me the gift of announcing, a bunch of times, for days, that he would be out on this particular Friday night, offering up the opportunity for me to have something to look forward to. Grayson's Pub, his second home, was unveiling the big screen television that had been delivered and installed on Tuesday but that Grayson aimed to use as a crowd-drawing event so he threw a sheet over it until the pay-per-view boxing match on Friday night. Even better, he had paid the $3 per person that Grayson was charging to cover the cost of pay-per-view for him, Michael, and David.

The minute I walked in from work on Friday night, Daddy stopped me. "Don't bother making dinner for me and the boys. We'll have a barbecue sandwich at Grayson's while we watch the big screen."

I grunted an answer so he'd hear a response because I wouldn't dare say what was on my mind, and headed off to my room to change out of my work clothes. He wasn't finished so he yelled the rest to me through my door.

"Your Mama's bath will have to wait until tomorrow night. After the boxing match, we'll probably stay and shoot a couple games of pool."

I think the alcohol finally ate away the last few brain cells he had left. I knew, as sure as my name was Clarice Marie McDaniels, the boys would traipse back in without him before his third beer. But I wasn't going to tell him that, or plan on one of them helping with the bath after they had a few beers.

Before they left, Daddy scared the liver out of Uncle Charles, his only brother, by calling him long distance – which wasn't even a thing anymore to anybody but them, since it was free – on a day that wasn't Christmas or his birthday. I could tell when he held the phone away from his ear that Uncle Charles was giving him an earful over that but Daddy went on bragging like the big screen belonged solely to him. If he had any way to win or steal that big screen away from Grayson, and a way to raise the roof on the trailer so it would fit, he would probably have moved the couch and Mama's end table out and stuck that thing right in front of the ugly recliner.

When he finally quit bragging to Uncle Charles and hung up the phone, and they all walked out, I sat on the bed beside Mama to talk about the party at Rena's. Since Emily got the wrong idea when I tried to talk to her about it, and I planned on waiting to tell her the rest until she resolved her anxiety about work and school, or my excitement settled down some and I didn't sound like a blooming idiot, I hoped Mama would understand, even if she couldn't let me know.

"Mama, these are nice rich people. I know you're probably wanting to tell me not to let dollar signs cloud up my vision, but you don't need to worry yourself over that. I'm not building pipe dreams about having a bunch of things that I don't need, or thinking Cinderella thoughts again." She didn't look at me but at least she wasn't hollering so it was easy for me to tell myself she was listening. "I guess the best part of it all is that Rena wants to be my friend, and she's a really nice person. I wish you could meet her. Today, she invited me to come to her apartment."

A knock on the front door interrupted my one-sided conversation. Out of respect, in case Mama was hearing me, I said, "Please excuse me, Mama, while I get the door."

We never had visitors other than David's friends and they mostly came during the day when they knew I wouldn't be around to tell them to take their feet off the couch or sit their chairs down on all four legs. I figured it was the boys coming back even earlier than I predicted. They didn't have enough sense between them to keep up with a key.

All the same, I peeked out the curtain like Mama always warned me to do before I opened the door. You could have knocked me over with a feather, because I never expected to see Emily standing there.

I wanted to tidy up the kitchen before I let her in, but there wasn't enough time to make a dent in the mess Daddy and the boys made while I was at work. Their breakfast and lunch dishes covered the table and counter, with food still on them. As soon as I opened the door, Emily would see it.

Whatever prompted her to stop by without warning me must have been important. Maybe she gave in and bought a junker after all, so she could drive herself to school. I opened the door a crack, thinking if she did buy the car she might take me out to see it without looking in at the messy kitchen. Or if Mama took to hollering, Emily might not hear on that side of the door.

She smiled a half smile and worked the other side of her mouth chewing away on her lip like something other than herself was really eating at her.

"This is a surprise." I said that like she didn't already know.

"I hope you don't mind, Clarice. Tracy drove me over here so I could ask a favor of you. Aren't you going to invite me in?"

I couldn't think up any excuse she would believe, so I opened the door and let her through. Emily plopped down in the recliner with a sigh; probably never guessing any home would have a piece of furniture off limits to all but one person. As far as the kitchen was concerned, she had picked the best spot because her back was to the mess.

I sat on the couch, straight across from the recliner, to keep her eyes from wandering around to the kitchen, and told her I would do any favor in my power for her.

"Did you mean it when you said you'd drive me to school? I'm thinking about your Mama. Doesn't she still have her heart problem and need you at home?"

"I can work around that," I told her, not sure how exactly but setting my mind on making my brothers take more responsibility.

Mama chose that very moment to let out one of the loudest, least recognizable words I'd heard from her that day. Emily jumped out of the recliner, screaming.

"It's okay," I said, hoping I sounded calmer than I felt. I tried to sit her back down in the chair and keep her eyes away from the kitchen. It wasn't okay at all, but Mama wasn't dying like I was sure Emily must have thought from the sound of things.

"She does that a lot," I said, realizing I needed to explain a lot more and hoping she wouldn't think I was nothing but a big liar.

"Em, Mama doesn't have a heart problem. She has something called dementia." The doctor called it dementia; Daddy and David called it plain fucking nuts.

"It's usually called senile dementia because it comes about when old people get too tired to remember everything. But Mama isn't old, so hers is just plain dementia."

Emily asked the million-dollar question. "What caused her to get it?"

I took a couple of deep breaths so I wouldn't start blubbering like a baby in front of her. Besides, if I really got going at it, I might never stop. Much as I loved Emily, I wished she wouldn't have just dropped by. I planned on telling her the truth about Mama as soon as I could do it without crying. The time hadn't come up yet.

"The doctor isn't sure what caused her to get it, and Dad said there's no use in dragging her around to a bunch of greedy specialists who'll confirm the same thing and soak up all his money in the meantime. So who knows? I have some thoughts on the subject, but I'm not a doctor."

Emily said she needed to run out front and tell Tracy she was going to be awhile. I wanted her to just go on home, but couldn't force those words out. I couldn't insult her by trampling all over her offer to listen to me whine about my Mama.

I saw a way out. "I understand if you need to go. We can talk about this another time when Tracy isn't waiting on you."

"Tracy won't mind if I ask her to go run her errands without me and come back later. I'll be right back." She left without giving me an option.

I ran to the kitchen and hid the dirty dishes in the oven while she was gone. Mama continued to holler, so I looked in on her to make sure she was okay and the lamp was on. Nothing in the pink glow looked out of place, she just took a notion to holler. "Emily came by, Mama," I said, in case she wanted me to finish the story about the party. "I won't be long."

I heard Tracy's car start up and went back to the living room to wait for Emily, thinking how good it would feel to have friends drop by if I lived in a normal home. I wanted to be like Rena, and have my own apartment where I could invite friends to come in for makeovers and not have to worry that my mother's dementia would kick in, or my brothers would come home and call us Cinderella. Even Emily had to worry about her dad keeping the windows closed up on hot nights and embarrassing her. Rena had it perfect, living alone.

Emily sat beside me on the couch when she came back, and picked back up, asking again what I thought caused my mother's dementia. I figured if anyone would understand, it had to be Emily, and finally didn't mind spilling my guts to her. But I wasn't sure Mama wanted me to spill hers to anyone.

Emily must have picked up on my thoughts. "Clarice, I promise you, nothing you tell me will ever leave my lips or change the way I feel about you or your mother. I remember what a nice lady she was."

So I explained the best I could. "I think this was Mama's only way out. She couldn't play the hand life dealt her any more. She knew she was going to lose, so she escaped the only way she knew how." Saying that right out was a little bit of a relief for me. Emily said that made sense to her, and poor mama.

"While I'm at it, I may as well tell you the rest." I didn't plan to say that, it just slipped out. I took it as a sign that I needed to empty everything out of my system while I had the chance.

"Emily, I get upset with her sometimes when I think about it. Why couldn't she be strong enough to look for a better life? She could have left him and found some kind of work to get by on. She could have been a singer. It's not like she would have been leaving much behind. Look around. This is it. The best he had to offer and she traded her mind for this."

I swung my arm dramatically, playing like tour guide the way Rena had, only pointing out the crap sitting around my home that was nothing like a museum.

"And she's not even allowed to sit in that recliner," I shouted.

Emily squinted her eyes a little and I couldn't tell if she was sad or afraid of me. She had to notice that I my sanity was skating close to the drop-off edge.

"She isn't allowed to sit in the recliner because she has dementia?" That seemed to piss Emily off almost as much as it did me.

"Long before she had dementia. None of us are allowed to sit there," I explained. "The king carted his throne in and sat it down there, taking up half the room. When he leans it back, there isn't room to squeeze between the chair and the cabinet and he won't move to let anyone through."

I was shouting, and I couldn't stop. "And no matter how tired Mama's legs were, or how many ornery boys were crowding up the couch and chairs, she wouldn't sit down in that recliner and prop her feet up. She just walked off upset, until it drove her to early dementia."

Emily was crying when I got finished and that made me even madder. My dad and his stupid chair were making people who weren't even kin to us cry.

As I predicted, David and Michael came through the door way too early, and looked at us on the couch – Emily crying like a baby and me right smack in the middle of a tirade. I ordered David to carry the recliner out front. "I don't ever want to see it again, David. Get it out of here."

Michael helped him. They carried the recliner down the road and left it in the dumpster sitting in back of the Otto's Produce.

We never saw the recliner again.

Emily practically ran out the door when Tracy pulled up beside my Escort out front.

She turned back to me once she was outside where she could breathe sane air. "You can come with us if you want, Clarice, and sleep over like old times."

"Thanks just the same, Emily. I can't leave Mama alone overnight. I'm sure the boys will drink more and things won't be pretty when Daddy gets here."

~~~

David took all of the blame on himself. He swore he had carried the recliner out front by himself, the same as he had all the other nights when he was in rare form. Probably, someone noticed it sitting out there and packed it off.

Michael and I sat on the couch with straight faces and let him do the talking. It's hard to say who would have been more upset if we contradicted him, David or Daddy, so we left it alone.

Daddy threw out the same old questions we'd heard a million and one times before. Do you think I was born yesterday? How stupid do I look? I was tempted to answer that one and get myself killed for sure. Which turnip truck did you see me fall off? He didn't believe David's story for a minute, but David stuck to it. That warmed my heart to David a little.

As far back as I could remember that was the first nice thing he had ever done for me. I say as far back as I can remember because Mama used to tell how David couldn't get his fill of me when I was a baby. He sang to me and shared his toys, and brought his friends home to see 'his' baby. How could anybody turn so different over time? She said young David told me I was beautiful, too; I just couldn't remember back that far.

It didn't matter that David took the blame; Daddy was upset with everyone out of principle. Anytime things didn't go his way, as a matter of his twisted principles, he thought the rest of the world deserved to suffer along with him.

He screamed about his ugly recliner most of the night. Mama kept up with him just about word for word, only hers weren't real words. At times, when his words sounded like her growls and hisses, I wondered if he was getting dementia too. I had half a mind to go get the chair and bring it back home myself, but it was too heavy for me.

Once, I started to scream out the truth because I couldn't stand the screaming. I wanted to tell him that Michael helped, and that it was all my idea in the first place, that I had told them to do it because that's what I think he deserves for not letting Mama sit down in it and put her feet up. But then he would have known David lied.

When he finally wore himself out and decided he wanted to get some sleep, he made David sleep on the couch and he took the bottom bunk under Michael. I wanted to smile at David so he'd know I appreciated him for taking the blame before I took off for Mama's room, but he wouldn't look up at me.

The McDaniels family resembled Emily's that night, except for the fact that the adults in her family actually liked each other – even after they were divorced. I had shut the window over the kitchen sink when Daddy took to screaming like a complete maniac. Usually, he used a hurtful tone that only sounded like screaming to us because we hated him, but the neighbors couldn't hear him. This time I figured the whole of Shady Acres must hear. Maybe the whole city.

And while Daddy slept in the boys' room, I crawled up in Mama's bed to console her. I whispered, not wanting to set Daddy off again if he was still awake. The sound of my voice either comforted her, or she had plain run out of hollering for once. Either way, she quieted down.

I whispered to her about David and Michael dumping the chair in Otto's dumpster, in case she couldn't hear when they told me where it ended up. I thought it might lighten up her dementia a bit to know that ugly chair was gone out of her living room for good. She did keep real still for a long spell after I told her, but it could have been coincidence.

I held her hand and whispered that Emily had asked about her when she dropped in but had to leave before she could make it back there to pay her a visit. Just in case she still had feelings that could be hurt. "Next time," I promised, "I'll be sure to bring her back."

Then it came to me. Emily came to ask a favor about me driving her to school. In all the commotion, I forgot to ask what the favor was. Some friend I turned out to be when push came to shove. She must have made the decision.

The neighbor frowned on personal calls, but I would call Emily first thing in the morning to apologize. I'd pretend it was a true emergency and I'd only keep her for a minute.

Mama pulled her hand away from mine and started acting restless. I told her about Emily wanting to go back to school, and then picked up on telling her about Rena inviting me to her apartment for a makeover.

"I know you don't want me to be vain, Mama. I don't plan on letting that happen. I'll keep my head about me, I just want to fix up a little bit and maybe find a husband someday to take me and you away from here." If she connected that to Cinderella, she didn't let on.

I whispered until I was hoarse and her eyes finally closed.

When I went into the kitchen next morning, I found David stretched out on the floor with a couch cushion under his head. He was a full foot longer than the couch and then some – almost as long as the room to be truthful. His head was right in the path of the door to the room where Daddy and Michael were sleeping.

I moved about the kitchen as quiet as a mouse, careful not to wake anyone while I cleaned up a space on the counter where I could make Mama's breakfast. But David stirred when the light from the refrigerator hit him in the face so I moved over a step to block the light while I returned the milk and butter to their places and closed the door quickly.

I stopped in the middle of slapping butter on her toast by the light that came in from the street lamp on the corner, and leaned my back against the refrigerator. If the door to the boys' room, on the far side of the living room, had been open, I would have had a bird's eye view of the faces in the bunk beds. I mentally paced off the distance. Ten steps across three rooms, and maybe another ten to the road out front.

We lived like the feeder mice at Reptile Supplies, crawling around on top of each other, never suspecting there was a whole world outside our tank that we could spread out in. No wonder Mama chose dementia over this.

My chest closed up on me. I had to get out of there. I finished the sandwiches and shoved them in the refrigerator without letting much light escape, dropped Mama's toast with jelly on her nightstand and planted a kiss on her cheek. After grabbing my purse from my room, I ran to the car before I smothered.

Chapter 10

When Clarice walked in on Monday morning, I knew immediately that something was terribly wrong. Not only was she late, dark circles upstaged the rhinestones and her demeanor suggested defeat.

She dropped her purse in the file cabinet drawer and nudged it shut with her knee, as though she didn't have the energy to offer the usual respect she gave furniture and equipment, not to mention her kindness to people. More significantly, she bypassed the coffee machine, climbed onto her stool without a cheerful good morning, and left her *closed* sign displayed.

I struggled with my emotions, and with a desire to handle the situation without escalating the pain that obviously dominated my friend. Each second I let pass felt like a thrash across the back of the friendship that I suddenly realized I had placed great importance on. My hand froze on the whip, afraid to let go until I saw some indication from Clarice that was what she wanted me to do.

Clarice forced a tight, lips-over-teeth smile, unaccompanied by eye contact.

"Will you cover the windows for a few minutes? Please."

In a voice laced with what I hoped was enough compassion to offset her resistance to eye contact or body language, I said, "Sure, Clarice. Take as long as you need."

Still presenting me with the unspiked but heavily-weighted-with-yesterday's-gel side of her head, she responded. "Thank you. No offense, but I need to make a personal phone call. I'm not clocked in yet."

The tables turned. Clarice took the whip from my hand and delivered a thrash with each step she took toward the pay phone in the lobby. Had my makeover suggestion caused this much pain? I wanted to ask Clarice that question, but realized the consequence might be the opposite of my intention. It could open the wound deeper.

Clarice returned from the phone and opened her window. She had worked on her hair while she was away and now had comb tracks running in straight lines through the gel. I interpreted that as a positive sign.

I convinced myself that it was better to try and fail than never try at all. "Is everything okay?" Apparently she didn't want to talk to me, and she didn't want to take a chance that I might overhear her talking to anyone else, but I wasn't going to let pride stand in the way. "You seem sad this morning, Clarice, and I want you to know I care."

She dropped her glasses on the counter and covered her eyes with her hands. I thought she was going to cry, and kicked myself again. I was like a black cloud she couldn't escape and apparently had finally blown her umbrella out of her hand.

In my concern for protecting Clarice from the humiliation of public tears, I forgot about my own aversion to them. Wiping the drops from my face proved to be a simpler task than trying to conceal my dripping nose. I went to the file cabinet to get tissues from my purse.

Her tiny voice caught me by surprise. "I sure hope you didn't mess with mascara this morning, Girlfriend."

I blew my nose before answering. "I knew there was a reason I didn't like that stuff. This is the perfect excuse for not wearing it."

"Do you cry often? I never picked up on that before."

"I hate to cry, Clarice, and usually refuse to let it happen in front of anyone. I'm not a very attractive crier. My face twists into a weird shape and my skin gets all splotchy."

"I'm sorry I didn't look while I had the chance," Clarice admitted. "It sounds entertaining. Are you okay now?"

With my crying to distract her, Clarice had forgotten to put her glasses back on.

"Your eyes are beautiful, Clarice. This is the first time I've seen them without your glasses. I never noticed how green they were before."

She showed the first slurpy smile of the day. "I got my Mama's eyes. They were her best feature."

That explained her reluctance to talk about her mother and the heart medication story. "I'm sorry. I thought your mother was still alive."

"She is," Clarice said.

"But you said were," I pointed out. "You said her eyes *were* her best feature."

"She's old now. They aren't as pretty as they used to be."

Clarice returned her glasses to her face and shuffled the statements on the counter in front of her. "We'd better get busy and make up for this time we've wasted."

We went to Jenky's for lunch, our first time there since the sweater incident. The new kid made sandwiches without dropping anything and Mrs. Jenky wore a tank top. We decided to put Jenky's back in our rotation, at least until sweater weather.

I tore the corner off my mustard package and noticed Clarice's lunch consisted of a glass of ice water and a bag of pretzels.

"Is that all you're going to eat? No sandwich?"

She shook her head. "I'm not hungry."

I withheld my opinion that she was already too thin, since it fell in the same category as the makeover and advice I had sworn away from lest I turn into my insulting, nagging mother.

"Do you want to talk about whatever is troubling you, Clarice? If it's something I've done, I want to know so I can make amends."

She dried her teeth with her lips and leaned in closer to the table. I hoped she was moving in closer to unload her deepest secrets, and not to tell me off without the rest of the diners hearing.

"You didn't do anything, Rena. I have some things troubling me at home, but I don't want to talk about them. No offense."

"I'm not offended," I said. "Maybe a little disappointed that you don't consider me a close enough friend to talk things over with, and a lot sad because I can't help if I don't know what's wrong, but I'm not offended."

Clarice popped a whole pretzel in her mouth and stared at the table while she chewed.

"I wasn't aiming to let you down or make you sad. There's nothing you can do about it, so I didn't see any point in dumping my garbage in your lap. Let's just talk about something happy. Let's plan the makeover."

Yesterday the makeover erased her seemingly permanent smile and today she classified it as a happy topic. Whatever happened to her overnight must have been horrible.

I apologized for my previous assumption that she would prefer that the makeover include only the two of us. "If you want, we can invite other friends and do the whole party thing." I rehashed the dorm party with Lori's mother, leaving out the fact that I was there as a hostile observer.

"My friend Emily and her sister might like to come," she said.

I said I would like to invite Jen.

"My mother doesn't get out much these days, but you could invite your mother. Not that she needs the help," she added quickly. "She might get a kick out of watching you get made over."

"I can ask her." I could only imagine the kick my mother would get out of watching both of us get made over. Maybe we could videotape the event for her collection of memorable accomplishments in her life. That thought made me fear she would invite media to capture her being motherly.

"Should we move this party to your house," I asked. "So your mother can make it?"

Clarice responded quickly and firmly. "No, your place is fine. If Mama feels up to doing anything when the time comes, I'll bring her. But don't count on it."

We ironed out the details of who and where easily. *When* posed more of a problem. Clarice had commitments every weekend and three nights during the week. She couldn't come right after work, and she needed to leave by nine. That left little to work with but it might take a while to find a makeover hostess with an available appointment on Wednesday or Friday, between the hours of seven and nine. I hoped it would be a long while. She would know I had tried and I would be off the hook.

Fate injects itself in places I never suspect. When I mentioned it to Jen, it turned out her boyfriend's cousin, Angela, sold some new line of cosmetics. A few phone calls later, she had said she would gladly give up a Friday evening to host an in-house party for Jen's best friend, and I was without an excuse. I accepted her offer of the last Friday of the month, which gave me two and a half weeks to prepare.

~~~

After confirming the date with Cousin Angela, I called Jen again to thank her for the referral. I also made her promise to help with the details since I didn't know how to plan a party without my mother's crew.

"Keep it simple," Jen advised. "You don't need a disc jockey or Betty running around with toilet paper. I heard about that and can't really say I'm sorry I skipped it. Just change the hand towel in the bathroom and set out a few snacks. You'll do fine."

"What kind of snacks?"

She laughed. "Cheap ones, of course. Whatever you like. I don't know. I can't believe you are doing this, much less stressing over details."

I couldn't believe it either. Jen was the one friend I had who might understand, so I explained briefly how I had cornered myself into planning this makeover.

"Is Clarice the girl you invited to your Mom's barbecue? My mother mentioned her. Is she really that bad?"

"She isn't bad at all." I hated being in the position to have to defend Clarice. No matter what I said, it would sound or feel wrong, like when a child pleads innocence and makes himself sound guiltier with every word.

"Clarice could use some orthodontic work, and better taste in eyewear, but she's really kind of cute. She has a body I'd kill for, although she seldom lets that show. You'll love her, Jen. She is, without a doubt, the most kind-hearted person I've even known."

"She sure had your mom in a tizzy. She called around trying to cash in favors to find help for the girl. I didn't think it would be as bad as it sounded third hand, through our mothers."

I felt embarrassed for Clarice again, even though she didn't know about Mother's calls.

Jen said she'd be around if I needed her. I almost felt excited about the party now that she was involved, but that feeling didn't last long. I went into a panic as soon as I hung up the phone.

Was Jen out of her mind? Change the hand towels? I didn't own a hand towel – but I would in two weeks. Stuffing junk in closets and closing the bedroom door wouldn't work if I had to invite Mother. Nothing short of a white-glove approved overhaul would do.

Pushing that thought aside, I went to the bathroom to examine my face under the fluorescent, let-me-show-you-every-flaw light. How much dirt did I have buried in my pores? Was I ready for the cotton ball expose?

Unless I learned to organize quickly, or took a two-week vacation from GWS, there was no way I could have my apartment and my pores ready for inspection in two weeks. I turned the incriminating lights out and went to my desk to start organizing.

I pictured Clarice with her clean pores, sitting somewhere in a Martha Stewart house, calling her friend Emily to beg her not to react when she examined my cotton ball. Anyone who successfully stretched an extra year out of her rose-colored blouse by updating the buttons could surely create a dollhouse on a shoestring, and produce a clean cotton ball on two-week's notice.

I tore a sheet of paper from my notepad and started a list. I needed to do three simple things - clean, decorate, and serve. I stared at the three words while I cleared the picture of Clarice and her perfect pores from my mind, and then erased decorate and serve and moved them to the bottom of the page. Now I had room to list each of my rooms as subcategories under the word clean: kitchen, dining area, living room, bedroom and bath. The apartment looked bigger on paper.

Problems arose immediately. There were things I needed to do, and things I needed to buy, for each room. I drew a vertical line down the center of the paper and proceeded to enter the dos on one side and the buys on the other.

A few major purchases came to mind. I turned the paper over and listed them separately. I needed a vacuum cleaner because mine didn't have attachments. The couch cushions and air vents still needed a thorough cleaning, even though Mother took the time to point out how filthy they were the last time she came by. Shame on her for not having a vacuum cleaner delivered post haste.

After carefully weighing the options, I chose giving Mother the satisfaction of gloating over her control over me to listening to her patronizing explanation of the merits of curtains. I added curtains on the buy side of my living room, bedroom and dining area subcategories, and put shower curtain in parentheses next to bathroom because I actually owned one and wanted to think more about replacing it.

With Martha Stewart's protégé on my guest list, I decided a tablecloth and candles were in order, and matching dishes a necessity. I didn't own four matching pieces of anything, and I needed seven if I planned to eat with my guests. I also needed serving dishes – small bowls for nuts and mints and at least one large bowl and platter.

I was getting somewhere. The tablecloth, candles, and china, the atmosphere would be more elegant than clinical and we might not feel like lab rats during the facial structure analysis.

Lori's Mom asked everyone to bring their own washcloths to her presentation. I didn't know if that was standard protocol, or out of necessity because fifty guests were expected. To be on the safe side, I added washcloths to the list so I could provide matching linens for my guests instead of requesting they bring them from home.

Should the washcloths match the hand towels and the hand towel the shower where they would eventually be kept, or the tablecloth on which they were to make their debut? I'd ask Jen what she thought.

I tore off a new sheet of paper and started a grocery list. Nuts and mints were easy; everything else caused problems. I wanted a cheese tray, but couldn't decide between fruit and vegetables to accompany it. I tried to remember what Clarice usually ordered at lunch, and couldn't picture her eating either. I put both on the list.

That left drinks and desserts, and my head still ached so badly from the fruit and vegetable decision that I couldn't make another decision. I left that for later, thinking Jen might ask Angela what went over well at her other parties.

Was the side table for Angela's cosmetic cases my responsibility? If Angela brought as much as Lori's Mom had, there wouldn't be room for all of it in my tiny dining area. Maybe I should buy card tables and folding chairs and set up in the living room.

A vision of the dorm girls bending over the plastic, fold-over mirrors Lori's Mom had provided flashed right along beside the memory of Clarice squinting to see when she removed her glasses. I added five lighted make-up mirrors to the major purchase sheet and hoped I could find a good sale.

I woke up several times during the night to add wine, flowers, and astringent to my list. This party would wipe out my savings.

Chapter 11

Emily wasn't upset with me for calling her at work. She said not to worry about the favor; she understood. "Anyone would get distracted if all hell broke loose at home like it had at your house. Shoot, with all that, I almost forgot the reason I dropped by myself. I still can't believe the boys carried the recliner out."

Since her favor indirectly concerned bank business, Emily stayed on the phone to tell me about it. Her manager offered her a chance to jump-start her education by attending a management-training program in the evenings. Tracy offered to drive Emily from her branch to the main office where the classes were held, and she had planned to ask me to pick her up there and drive her home when they were over.

"But seeing how your mother needs you at home now, I won't ask you to do that. I'll work something else out, or wait until I get the car." She tried not to let me hear her disappointment.

"Tell them you'll be there, Emily. As long as I have time to run home and check in on Mama, I can pick you up." I didn't want to tell her I had to change a diaper. For Mama's sake, and mine, I kept that secret.

Emily said she loved me and she'd make it up to me one day.

Rena suspected something was wrong, and her feelings were hurt because I didn't tell her what it was. What was I supposed to say? Friday night I lost control and ordered my brothers to cart Daddy's ugly recliner out to punish him for driving my mother plain fucking nuts, but I'd still like to come to your apartment for a makeover? Hardly the way to make friends with someone who thinks her mother has a problem because she had a facelift.

David was alone with Mama when I got home on Monday. I walked through the kitchen, trying not to look at the mess, and dropped my shoes and purse in my room before I went to change her and tell her about my day, more to keep my mind off everything than because I thought she wanted to hear.

During the screaming on Friday night, and during the time I spent wasting breath afterwards, it finally sank in. Mama didn't listen to anything I said. I could believe that babies took in more than they gave back, but I gave up believing that was true about my mother. Diapers were all she had in common with babies; Mama wasn't moving forward.

I asked David if he knew whether or not Daddy and Michael would be there to eat. Knowing how many hamburgers to fry or pork chops to bake got harder all the time.

When he finally looked up, he didn't look like he hated me for once. "The old man's out looking for his chair. He's been at it all day, harassing the neighbors and threatening to call the police."

I held back a giggle, figuring it wouldn't be good to push David's civil mood.

"Michael went up to Otto's early this morning and the chair was gone. The dumpster was empty and the recliner nowhere around. So it ain't coming back. I don't know where he went after that. He hasn't been back either."

"I'm sorry he took your bed," I said. "I wasn't aiming for anything like that to happen."

I didn't know what to make of the way David looked back at me. He still wasn't angry. His eyes weren't exactly soft, but they definitely weren't angry. He didn't look like himself.

"Thanks for taking the blame all on yourself." I smiled, thinking he might be on the verge of nice.

"Don't flatter yourself, Cinderella. I carried the recliner out of here because I wanted to, not because you told me to.

"I appreciated it all the same."

I started toward the refrigerator, aiming to take three hamburger patties out, but David grabbed my arm and stopped me. I didn't struggle with him. I dropped my head, too tired to even be upset. "What do you want, David? I need to get dinner."

He kicked the leg of the chair across from him, shoving it out from under the table, and asked me to sit down. He didn't actually say 'Clarice will you please sit down', but the way he said 'sit down, sounded more like a question than an order, so I did as he asked.

"Why do you do this?" He sounded angry, but his face still looked a little bit nice.

"I'm sorry, David. I didn't aim to do anything to upset you." That wasn't the answer he was fishing for.

He slammed his fist on the table, causing Mama to holler when she heard the crash. I pushed my chair back and he reached across the table to grab my arm again.

"Sit still." That one was an order.

"You won't change a damned thing trotting your ass back there to turn on lava lamps or whisper stories in her ear every time she yells. Not a God damned thing, Clarice. She's plain fucking nuts. The sooner you get that through your thick skull, the better off you'll be."

I didn't want to listen, but his face still lacked the usual anger and I didn't want to let go of that either. My glasses fogged up from the heat coming off my face mixing with the tears I was fighting with all my might to hold inside. I put the glasses on the table and wished I could turn my hearing off as easily as I had my vision. Mama's screaming was wearing on my last nerve.

"She needs me, David."

He slammed his fist down again, this time sending my glasses flying over into the living room. They landed where the recliner used to be.

"She needs a lot of things, Clarice, but you ain't one of them. She needs a brain and a backbone. She needs to get over letting some jackass ruin her life, and ours along with it. She needs her husband to change the shitty diapers, not you. You clean her, you feed her, and you pay her bills. That's not how it's supposed to be. He's the one that married her – he should take care of her."

"I raise her sons, too," I reminded him. "I feed you and keep a roof over your head and water in your toilet just the same as I do for her." I couldn't believe I had the nerve to say all of this. "Now, I need to get up from here and clear the mess out so I can make dinner before her screaming drives me plain fucking nuts, too."

I threw my chair back on the floor and jerked the refrigerator door open with such energy that the ketchup and mustard bottles flew off the shelf in the door and crashed at my feet. I surprised myself again by having the second temper tantrum of my life jump out on me just one day after the first, and hoped it wasn't going to be a habit.

David picked the condiments up and sat them on the dirty counter without saying a word. Then he went to the living room to get my glasses and hand them to me.

I said thank you, thinking it was a crying shame he started liking me on the very day I hated him the most. It was too late for me and David. I had to shut myself off from warming up to him because he played with my feelings too much when he jumped back and forth from the verge of nice to ripping my heart out with mean words about Mama.

Mama kept on hollering. I looked at the mess again, and thought about what David said, and I remembered the look on Rena's face when she asked if it was something she had done. Disappointment came at me from every direction until I knew it was more than I could hold inside. I let it slide out on tears. There must have been close to a million and one tears running down my face. And they felt good.

David looked at me like he was scared. He must have figured I went off the deep end just like Mama and Daddy, since I was standing there in the kitchen blubbering on like that instead of hiding in my room where he couldn't see.

It worked in my favor. "You start cooking and I'll work on the cleaning," he said, taking the dirty dishes off the counter next to the stove to make room for me to get dinner. David washed dishes and I fried hamburgers while I finished my cry.

I fried his hamburger, but left it in the skillet instead of serving it up on a bun with lettuce and mustard the way he liked. I went half way, just like he did when he tried to be nice to me.

Mama calmed down after she ate and I changed her for bed. I didn't spend much time talking to her. Because I was too tired, not because David told me to stop talking to her.

Michael came in and told us he took a job on the barge. He'd be gone for weeks at a time which, he said, sounded like heaven to him. Daddy didn't come home, and that was like heaven to me.

I dreamed about Highway 24 that night. I drove in and out, seeing things in detail like I had the day after Rena's party. Shady Acres lived in eternal darkness; dark when I pulled out and dark when I came back, like on workdays in the winter. When I got as far as Otto's, the sun peeked out. The further I went out the road, the more things changed. The sun got brighter, and the trees had more leaves, and the road seemed wider and I felt more at home.

One day, I just knew it in my heart, I was going to drive off and never return.

Chapter 12

The already faltering confidence I had in my ability to organize this makeover took a nose dive when I picked up my lists and realized that not everything could be done ahead of time. My first contribution to the party – my list of things to do - required immediate revision.

I concentrated on my pores and shopping the first week, visiting different stores each night before coming home to cleanse, steam, tone and moisturize. Before going to bed each night, I reorganized the lists by date, hoping to squeeze everything in without using vacation days or having a nervous breakdown. I learned two things about myself that week. My pores were remarkably clean despite the years of neglect, and I possessed an innate decorating talent that I never suspected was there.

A fuzzy layer of steam-baked dust on the medicine cabinet caught my attention while I examined my pores one morning. I sighed, realizing the whole room needed to be scrubbed from top to bottom. In the process of estimating the time that would take so I could update the list, I found a reason to appreciate the eggshell colored walls and floors that had almost turned me against the apartment in the first place. Without painting anything, I could change the bathroom to match the living room and dining area, and solve the color-coordination problem with the hand towels and wash clothes.

I grabbed my list from the back of the toilet – having learned to keep it close at hand over the last few days – and rearranged the schedule. I returned the green hand towels and washcloths that I had already bought to match the bathroom, and exchanged them for a shower curtain in the exact shade of pale yellow as the vertical stripe in the maroon wallpaper on the dining room wall. I also found table cloths that matched the towels and washcloths.

I left my collection of yellow white-sale items lying out on the dining room table so I could admire how beautifully they matched the wallpaper, and so I would remember to ask Clarice if she thought white-sale was as inappropriate a title as sweater was. I almost surprised myself by hoping Mother would notice how perfectly I matched everything without me having to point it out.

Even if Mother wouldn't, Jen congratulated me on a job well done when she saw the yellow collection. She also suggested I add some color. She took me to Pier One Imports, where we found maroon candles and serving dishes and she talked me into a matching rug for the entrance and pillows for the couch – things that weren't on the list or in the budget. I protested in the store, but thanked her when we got home and I saw how they pulled everything together.

I shopped alone after that but found myself turning to other customers and sales representatives for help. Sometimes they noticed me wandering around in a state of confusion and offered; and sometimes I went to them with questions. The six make-up mirrors I loaded into my cart on my third trip to Bed Bath & Beyond extracted special attention from a fellow shopper, who ended up helping me find curtains.

The lady approached me with a chuckle. "I hate to be nosy, but curiosity is killing me. Is there a sale on make-up mirrors?"

"I hope so, but I haven't seen it advertised if there is," I answered. "I'm hosting a makeover, and wanted my guests to be able to see their faces."

The lady said she also hated the tiny mirrors provided at makeovers and thought it was very considerate of me to provide bigger ones for my guests. "I'm just curious, though. Where are you going to plug them all in?"

I hadn't thought of that, and said I was glad she brought it up. She suggested I use a power strip under the table and walked with me through the store to look for one. She stopped when the curtains distracted me, and helped me select window coverings for the three rooms that needed them. I asked her to join us for the party, but she declined, saying she didn't want me to have to buy another mirror and washcloth.

The most fun I had shopping was at Target. Jansen Ames found me staring hopelessly at a row of vacuum cleaners and offered to help.

"I need something with attachments that I can use to clean upholstery and heat vents." I looked past him to the prices listed below the display. I had already spent more than I planned when I bought the shower curtain and rug and pillows, and hoped to get by with an inexpensive vacuum cleaner. "I can't afford anything expensive."

Jansen demonstrated each model, explaining special features that made one better than the other. He checked for warranties, and priced replacement bags and belts, and told me which models sold the most and which he thought were the best buys. I thought of Clarice, and how she had explained the pride she felt in her customer service position. This guy devoted the same level of dedication to the customer as he assisted me.

"Target is lucky to have you," I told him. "I came here knowing very little about vacuum cleaners and you have patiently explained everything I needed to know in order to make a wise choice."

He thanked me for noticing, and offered to take my selection to the checkout lane for me. On the way there, I asked how long he had worked at Target and where he went to school, trying to determine his age. I thought he was about my age, which would also be Clarice's age, and didn't see a wedding band. I wrote his name on the bottom of my list.

On the weekend before the party, I scrubbed the bathroom and hung the shower curtain so the smell of new plastic would fade before the party. I hung the curtains; disappointed to find that I had to wash the windows first because I couldn't force myself hang new curtains over dirty windows.

At the end of the day, I sat on the couch to rest and enjoy the new curtains and another mysterious wave of domesticity overcame me. I couldn't relax until I vacuumed the upholstery. I unpacked the new vacuum cleaner and used the attachments that Jansen had demonstrated. The room looked nice.

I took the easy way out and ordered the cheese, fruit, and vegetable trays from the deli at the grocery store so I could pick them up on my way home from work on Friday and they would be fresh. Jen offered to help shop for the rest of the food and drinks on Thursday night, and to help set everything up so I wouldn't have much left to do on Friday before the party.

We unpacked the folding table I bought to sit between the dining room table and living room for Angela to put her cases on. I broke the box down and leaned it against the door. Jen stared at me like I was a stranger.

"I can't believe you bought all of this stuff for a make-up demonstration," she said. "I had a jewelry party once and I just bought chips and dip and sodas. I think I dusted the night before, and that was it."

I spread the yellow tablecloths on the tables and bent down to plug the power strip in and place it under the table. "I have to admit, I went overboard. But I really did enjoy the preparations. Weird, huh? I won't enjoy the Visa bill when it comes."

"Don't forget, you still have to buy make-up. That's the whole purpose of all this."

I hadn't even thought of that part. I planned the party to see if Clarice wanted to change her appearance, and I probably wouldn't even know the answer to that question after all of this was over.

Jen stayed until we had everything ready. The tables looked nice with the mirrors and tablecloth and matching candles and washcloths.

I decided to buy maroon napkins to replace the washcloths after the party, and maybe something yellow for the kitchen, to tie it in with the dining room.

Jen hugged me good-bye and picked up the table box to drop it in the dumpster on her way out. "I hope Clarice has as much fun with this as you have. You're a good friend, Rena."

Jen understood.

Chapter 13

Michael called the jail first because that seemed the most likely place for Daddy to be when he was gone this long. We figured he could still be obnoxious enough to get arrested, even without his car. They didn't have him.

He called the bars next, then the hospitals, and finally Daddy's friends. Nobody knew where he was, or even acted concerned from what I gathered from Michael's report. Not a single person said to call back if we found him so they'd story worrying.

I called Uncle Charles in Georgia, mostly out of curiosity. He said Daddy better not waste his time coming up there because he would send him packing so fast his head would spin. "He ain't never been nothing but trouble and I don't see him changing any time soon," were his exact words.

I can't say as I blame Uncle Charles for holding hard feelings. Daddy never called just to ask *how are you*, and he forgot to ask about Aunt Judy when she had her operation. Uncle Charles said that was the final straw as far as he was concerned and washed his hands of our whole family. He didn't ask how I was, and I didn't tell him about Mama, figuring he wouldn't want to know just to get even for Daddy not asking after Aunt Judy.

We decided Daddy ran away; skipped out on his demented wife just like the creep we always knew he was. Michael wanted to call the police and report him missing, but he didn't have the gumption to do it on his own and David and I sure weren't going to do it. I figured it was one less mouth to feed, one less person to clean up after, and a whole lot more peace. Good riddance as far as I was concerned.

Mama didn't seem to notice Daddy was gone.

When I broke the news to the boys about agreeing to pick Emily up after her management classes twice a week, and would need them to look after Mama, they carried on like I had asked them to pack her clean up a steep hill on their backs and watch her forever. The whole trip – from Shady Acres to the main office downtown, and from there to Emily's house on Paine Avenue, and then back to Shady Acres – took just over an hour. All I asked them to do was stay there with her for one measly hour when they didn't have anything else to do anyway. And listen if she hollered, which they had to do even when I was there, so that was nothing.

Since they acted like such big fools over something as important as Emily getting home from school, I figured on the fight of my life when I asked them to watch Mama on a Friday night so I could go to Rena's party. I pulled myself up strong and used my old trick of making believe my life depended on what I was fixing to say. "I need you to look after her for a couple hours on Friday, too."

David must have thought it was his job, as the oldest child in the family, to take up Daddy's matter of principle thinking now that he skipped out. David never left the house before ten on a Friday night, but out of principle, he had to give me a hard time.

"What's the deal with this Rena and her parties? You need to tell that girl you aren't a social butterfly and you have responsibilities at home. It's your job to take care of Mom at night."

"No, my job is to work at the customer service window at the gas company forty hours a week. They pay me for that. Getting paid makes it a job. The last party was a month ago. You get out more than once a month. Why shouldn't I?"

Michael didn't say anything, but I thought he looked more upset with David than he did with me.

"Because I take care of her all day." David's tone was harsh. "And I don't get paid a red cent for any of it so I guess it ain't my job anymore."

"You *stay* with her all day, maybe." I made sure my tone was as harsh as his. "You don't fix her meals or change her. You probably don't even look in at her except when you take her the lunch I fixed before I left for my job." I raised my voice even louder on the last two words. "And you do get paid. You live here rent free, and you eat the food I buy."

"What kind of party is it?" Michael asked.

I explained about the makeover, and that I wouldn't be out late, getting angry with myself as I spoke. Mama wasn't my total responsibility; David said so himself when he was talking about Daddy being the irresponsible one. I didn't need to ask anyone's permission to go out. I was an adult.

"Forget I asked you," I said. David grinned like he won the fight. "I'm telling you, not asking you. I have plans Friday night so one of you needs to be here with Mama. Talk it out between you and decide."

David started to grumble over it, but Michael interrupted. "You made fun of her all those years. It looks like you'd be happy now that she wants to go to this makeover thing and learn to fix herself up." He turned to me. "I'll be here, Clarice, so you don't need to worry."

David huffed and tried to still sound kind of mean. "Michael makes a good point. Guess it would be good for you to learn how to fix up that ugly face so we don't have to look at it anymore."

I knew he only said that so he could throw the hurt back in my face instead of admitting that he was wrong, or that he was giving in. I pretended it didn't hurt. My first inclination was to say thank you, but I bit my tongue to keep it back. The reason they thought Mama was my responsibility was because I acted like they were doing me a favor when they did something for her.

"She belongs to you as much as she does to me," I said. "And so does the trailer. You could start taking care of it and cleaning your own messes, too."

That settled things as far as I was concerned. I took that as a sign that the party was meant to be – destiny sort of. At first, I thought Rena would change her mind since she had told me she hated those things. But she surprised me and set it all up. She even seemed excited about it.

Then, I thought I would have to make an excuse because I didn't have any money to spend. I knew the make-up lady expected to sell something if she took the time to come out and show us her products, so I didn't want to waste her time if I couldn't buy anything. But the lady came back to pay me for covering her balance and I ended up with thirty dollars to spend. The boys were the last obstacles and here they were coming through.

When all was said and done, I wondered if I really wanted to go after all. I wanted to go to Rena's apartment and meet her friend, but I didn't want everybody gawking at me while I put on make-up. Maybe they would be too busy watching Emily because she was so pretty.

I could always say Mama needed me, but then I'd have to explain why to Rena and I knew I couldn't do that. Maybe I would chicken out and say I was allergic to cosmetics or something, and just watch the others do their facials.

Those were just crazy thoughts, though. I knew in my heart I would end up going.

Chapter 14

The deli arranged the food beautifully, on flimsy aluminum platters that were difficult to handle even though they looked nice enough. I transferred the fruit and vegetables on the maroon, Pier One platters, and the cheese on the single crystal plate I inherited when no one claimed it after a potluck at the dorm, covered everything with plastic wrap and put it in the refrigerator.

After I added two dishes, one with nuts and the other with mints, the table was ready except for lighting the candles. Why didn't I think to pick up a camera on one of my shopping trips? Dad would have to see this to believe I pulled off anything so close to smart.

I checked each room against the list, inspecting carefully for anything I might have missed or failed to put on the list in the first place. Everything was perfect, except the bedroom, and I planned to close the door so no one could see it – knowing that Mother wouldn't be able to resist a peek.

I had an hour left before Angela arrived and needed every minute to get myself ready. A last minute panic hit when I realized I didn't know what to wear for this occasion. My dorm makeover probably wasn't typical and it was my only experience. My guest list offered no protocol.

Mother would show up, late, in a silk pantsuit that clung intentionally to accent her most expensive body parts. Jen wore jeans everywhere, adjusting them to go from work to a wedding by changing shoes and tops.

I didn't know Emily or her sister, but assumed they would be as much like Clarice as Jen was like me. But assumptions, I reminded myself, are dangerous. Mother and I disprove the assumption that people are the same because they come together or are associated in some way. Would Clarice come as the Clarice I knew at GWS, or the Clarice I met at Mother's barbecue? As the hostess, did anyone expected me to present a particular image?

I mulled it over while I steamed my face and gave it one last cotton ball test before the big production, and decided on jeans for Jen, a tan silk pullover shell for mother, and leopard skin mules in case Clarice arrived in her barbecue persona. I added a hint of mascara and lipstick so I would have something to cleanse off to prove I was willing to bare it all along with my guests.

Why was I so obsessed with making this so right? With a few minutes to spare, I waited on the couch, barely breathing lest I blow dust on the clean upholstery or collect it in a pore.

Angela convinced me I must have a fairy godmother or at least a lucky star. My apprehension slipped out the door when she came through it and presented herself as the exact opposite of Lori Zeller's mother.

I tilted my head back to meet her spirited, raven eyes with my own relieved ones. By my calculations, that made her at least six feet tall in the flat boots I wanted to own as soon as I saw them standing on the maroon rug in front of my door.

She made herself at home, shoving her things under the table that she correctly assumed was for her use, or claimed without the assumption. "I see you've been busy. This is lovely," she said, looking at my over-adorned table. "You're the first person I've seen use lighted make-up mirrors. This is excellent."

What a relief. "I was afraid it was too much."

I quickly explained about the one makeover I had witnessed, and the customer at Bed Bath & Beyond, who kindly laughed at me for going to extremes, and how important it was to me that I get this party right. I finished my spiel, out of breath and totally embarrassed.

Angela's eyes assured me as much as her smile did. "I think you've done a wonderful job, and this will be a very successful makeover. You just relax and enjoy yourself now. I do the work and worry from this point on."

She sat me in a chair to watch and listen as she opened her bags to set up.

"I guess I won't need my tablecloth or mirrors. You've done so much of my work for me already," she said, stacking catalogues and color charts and supplies on the folding table. "Before your guests arrive, I'll tell you what seems to work best. Don't serve food or drinks until we have completed the makeover, because sometimes that encourages long discussions about recipes, or you end up with a spill that interrupts the flow. You become a guest and I'm the hostess until the demonstration ends. I'll clue you when it's time for refreshments."

As she made arranging what seemed like a hundred small items with less effort that it had taken me to place my few items on the table, I took it all in, slightly distracted by the grace with which she made every move. I tried to remember if I had ever seen anyone more beautiful than Angela and came up blank, then noticed that she was wearing very little make-up. That seemed odd since she was there to promote a line of cosmetics.

Her overall appearance was very natural, but striking at the same time. She struck the balance I had always wished for in clothing, with a simple, mid-calf length brown skirt and an oversized tan blouse belted at the waist. Her hair, pulled into a barrette at the neck, hung in a silky black ribbon that almost met the belt; and her caramel skin was radiant enough on its own that it would have outshone jewelry had she worn any.

Mother! Fortunately, that shout was internal only. Mother! replaced the typical Uncle! as I surrendered the pain that usually accompanied admitting that I was thinking like Mother.

"For inviting me into your home," Angela said, drawing me back to reality, "you get a set of sable cosmetic brushes and ten percent of the party total to use toward your purchase." She sat my brand new, never before even remotely coveted leather vase of brushes in the center of the table for display. "If I book another party with one of your guests, you receive your choice between a higher discount on your order and a selection from our gift catalogue. I'll show that to you when I'm finished here."

I didn't know I received benefits for asking my friends to humiliate themselves publicly. That information drudged back the apprehension. I wanted to understand Clarice, not use her for personal gain.

"Suppose I want to offer my discount to one or my guests instead of using it on my own purchase. Could that be arranged?"

Angela stopped arranging brushes and sponges at place settings and pulled herself up straight to look at me before she answered. "I could arrange that if you want. However, it would be in your best interest to ask you guest to host her own party. Actually, her best interest too, because she would receive the hostess gift and have the opportunity to divide her purchase into two paychecks. This line is a little expensive so many hostesses appreciate that opportunity."

I said I would think about it before I made a decision.

Jen arrived next, twenty minutes early in case I needed help. She wore the jeans I had predicted, with a pink satin blouse that made her blonde hair glisten, and open-toed pumps to show off her pedicure.

"Wow, Rena, this place looks great," she said, handing over a bottle of Martini and Rossi Asti Spumante. "Here, I thought we might need this later, to celebrate our new found beauty, or drown the anger you feel toward your mother. Your choice."

Angela voted for the celebrated beauty.

"You haven't been around Rena and her mother," Jen warned. "It gets tense. Please, Rena, try to be civil. Ignore her if you have to."

I promised to do my best.

Clarice, Emily, and Tracy came in together, although they had driven two cars. Clarice wore her rose-colored blouse with the new buttons, tucked into khaki Capri pants – somewhere between the work and barbecue persona. Her hair was freshly gelled and spiked. Emily and her sister, Tracy, represented opposite ends of the spectrum. Emily wore a navy business suit and Tracy wore as little as possible. I decided to seat her on the side of the table away from the air-conditioning vent in case we had to turn it on, which would be quite possible with so many people crowded into my tiny space.

Angela suggested I sit at the end of the table by the kitchen so I could get in and out easily to answer the door or phone or get to the kitchen if we needed something. She recommended turning the phone off once all of the guests had arrived. Jen sat next to me on the wall side of the table, with Clarice on the other side of her. The sisters sat across from them, leaving the other end of the table vacant for Mother.

"Should we wait?" Angela asked. "For your mother to arrive?"

"It's your call," I answered. "Mother is always late, and when she comes in, you'll have to stop while she makes her grand entrance. Go ahead if you don't mind being interrupted, or wait if you'd rather."

Jen kicked me under the table, but I knew she knew I was right.

"We'll give her a few more minutes," Angela decided.

Strained small talk held us over. Emily and Tracy answered direct questions but offered nothing else. Clarice told me everything looked nice and thanked me for inviting her. Jen said she was starving because she didn't have time to eat before she came, and she couldn't wait to dig into the cheese ball. I wished Mother would hurry up and arrive.

She came fifteen minutes late. I let her in and walked back to the table where everyone else waited. She went the opposite direction, into the empty living room and pirated another ten minutes of what she must have considered our inconsequential time.

She wore a silk pantsuit, snug in the right spots, and expensive enough to be called eggplant instead of purple, with matching shoes and purse, and diamonds on her fingers, wrists, earlobes and neck. Congratulations, Mother, you win the door prize for having the biggest breasts, the most expensive clothes, the highest heels, and for wearing more carets than the rest of us will ever own collectively. And every eye in the room is on you.

"Rena, dear, I'm positively speechless. How quaint." She wasn't wearing white gloves but she did touch the couch and the curtains. I wished I had thought to buy a step stool so she could reach the vent. "I never dreamed you could turn this little place into anything nearly so lovely."

Apparently, she didn't know that speechless meant without word.

She returned to the curtains and rolled the hem of one between her fingers, probably confirming her worst fear – they were cotton. "They do add some warmth to the white walls and floor." She looked around, taking in the whole room. "As much as I hate to admit it, you were probably right to use curtains with that short sofa, instead of full draperies as I would have used."

I said thank you so we wouldn't have speechless in common.

"I apologize for being late. Judge Harris caught me at the last minute and I couldn't escape without appearing to be rude. He wanted my opinion on a paper he is writing, as if I'm some sort of expert. Bless his heart, I looked it over and he desperately needed my help. You'll forgive me for not letting him down."

How about letting your kid down? I wondered who she could order to do that. She turned toward us, building false hope that she had finished.

"And then, of course, I still wanted to run home and change into something more casual before I came here. I didn't want to look like a haggard old lady in front of my daughter and her cute little friends."

Angela cast me an understanding smile. Jen squeezed my hand until she cut off my circulation.

Once she mentioned friends, she was forced to acknowledge her captive audience. "Jen, dear, you look wonderful. The last time I saw you, you were in a cast and you looked so tired. I'm glad to see you are feeling better. Clarice, it's great to see you again, dear."

Clarice introduced Emily and Tracy to Mother, and I introduced Angela, our hostess, trying to remind her of the reason we were gathered around my table with mirrors and washcloths.

Mother distributed plastic compliments with all the finesse of a casino dealer passing out an even number of cards face down so only the recipient knows their true value. Finally, she settled into her seat at the opposite end of the table from mine to grudgingly share the spotlight with Angela.

We turned our mirrors on while Angela dispensed a few drops of cleansing cream on each of our pallets and stressed the importance of proper skin care. "I promote our skin care line more than I do the cosmetics because I believe if you have clean, healthy skin, the rest isn't as necessary.

Mother leaned over to speak to Clarice. "Listen to her dear. This is excellent advice."

Angela took a deep breath. "Now, if you will dip the end of your ring finger into your cleansing cream, I will demonstrate the proper technique for cleansing, and explain how it protects your skin from stretching."

Everyone but Mother dipped. She said she had been through the demonstration more times than she could count. Obviously, she thought her time would be better spent interrupting Angela and overseeing every move Clarice made.

I wondered if it would be more appropriate to return her mirror and say it was unused, or to ask her to reimburse me for the money I wasted on her. She answered the question for me by studying her face each time Angela mentioned wrinkles, thereby removing my unused option.

Clarice indulged Mother's doting; she even asked her advice the few times it wasn't forced on her without asking. Mother told Clarice to call her Charlotte, giving Jen a start, and leaving Emily and Tracy to wonder if they were to do the same. Confusion and tension permeated the room more intensely than the scent from my Pier One candles.

I experimented with different shades of eye shadow, deciding, with Angela's assistance, on a neutral shade that smoothed my skin tone more than it colored, duplicating Angela's natural look. Thinking I had reached the level of perfection I wanted before I asked my guests for final approval, I looked up from my mirror and forgot my mission. Clarice beat me to perfection.

I nearly screamed her name. "Clarice, you look beautiful."

The other heads came up from their mirrors. "Look at her eyes," I said.

Emily and Tracy raved in unison, as I imagined sisters who share secrets and emotions often do.

"She's right, Clarice. You are beautiful." Emily sounded as pleased as I felt.

Clarice showed all of her teeth and wiped the corner of her mouth with a tissue. Mother backed away. "If you guys are aiming to butter me up for favors later, you're on the right path. Keep it up."

"Seriously, Clarice, your eyes are mesmerizing," Angela told her. "You've done a wonderful job with colors. You are beautiful."

Clarice grabbed her glasses from the center of the table and put them on, detracting from the perfection but at least she could see it for herself. "I can't see so good without my glasses. Let me take a better look."

She studied her mirror while we studied her reaction, and then she turned to hug Mother. "Charlotte picked these colors out for me and helped me get them in the right places. It's all her doing."

"No, dear," Mother said. "You came in here with beautiful eyes. I only helped you discover them."

I waited for the backside of the compliment, but it never came. Mother allowed Clarice her time alone in the spotlight. I almost hated my mother for cheating me of my expectation, but was too happy for Clarice to let that feeling settle into place.

Jen and Emily approved my color choices, and I theirs. We all knew it was futile to try and talk Tracy out of her gaudy colors.

Angela gave me the refreshment cue and I excused myself, hoping someone would use the bathroom and vindicate my Visa bill. I removed the plastic covered trays from the refrigerator while Angela helped with orders.

Angela and I cleared the mirrors and makeover supplies from the table. She packed her bags and helped with orders, and Jen helped me put the food out and fix drinks.

When the orders were complete and Angela had tallied the total, she came to speak to me. "The party went well, and I want you to keep the discount for yourself. You earned it."

"Thanks for noticing, but I want to make sure Clarice can get the eye make-up."

"I don't think that will be a problem," Angela assured me. "Clarice will get what she wants."

I figured Mother had let Angela know she had that covered.

"Don't forget the Asti," Jen whispered. "We can use it for both purposes. You controlled yourself well, and you look great."

Emily booked the next makeover at her house, three weeks later so she could be sure the weather would have cooled off. "This is perfect," Clarice announced. "I ordered the eye colors tonight and I can get the cleansing system at Emily's party."

"And then you can book the next party after Emily's and get the rest," Mother suggested, making me wonder if I had guessed wrong.

Mother finished gushing over Clarice, used the bathroom and checked my room so she would have one legitimate criticism, and said she needed to get home and spend time with Dad. I walked her to the door before she could change her mind.

Clarice ran around the table and caught Mother on the way out the door. "Thanks again, Charlotte. I'll call you tomorrow."

Jen was beside me with a glass of Asti. She shoved it in my hand. "Cheers, Rena. Come sit down and unwind. I have a great idea."

She poured drinks for everyone then presented her plan. "Since we're all dressed up and looking so good, I think we should make this a real ladies' night out. Let's go somewhere."

Chapter 15

Emily fastened her seatbelt. "You really do look great, Clarice. Your eyes could be on a magazine cover or something."

"Thanks, Em. I had fun at the party. I hope I can remember how to put this stuff on when mine comes in, so I can do it without Charlotte sitting there telling me every move."

That was true, but what concerned me the most at that moment was Mama. I didn't want to have to worry about her, or my brothers, or my missing father. On November 2, I would turn twenty-four, old enough to be married and have my own children. Old enough to go out with my friends without asking anyone's permission. Old enough to make my own decisions.

"Emily, do you think we're too old to keep on living with our parents? Look at Rena. She's our age and she has the same job as me, and she has her own apartment and her own life. Do you think about leaving Paine Avenue?"

Emily turned the radio on and scanned until she found a song she liked. "I think about it sometimes, but I know if I moved out I wouldn't be able to save any money. Rena's parents probably bought her a car and maybe some furniture and stuff, and she knows if she runs into a problem down the road, they can help her out. It's easier for someone like her. Know what I mean?"

I did know. Rena's mother offered to buy my make-up and I'm not even kin. I didn't let her buy it, even though I knew it wouldn't hurt her in any way to do it. Rena had security that I'd never know, and she didn't even seem to appreciate it. I didn't understand her sometimes.

"You make a good point, Em. Rena doesn't know how lucky she is to have Charlotte for her mother. Her Dad's real nice too."

"It depends on how you look at things," Emily said. "Charlotte could be a real pain in the butt if you ask me. I felt sorry for Rena tonight. Her mother was rude to her."

Nobody got it except me. Charlotte showed off a little; Mama hollered constantly. Charlotte dressed like a floozy; Mama wore Depends under the ragged nightgowns that she was stuck wearing day and night. Charlotte annoyed Rena by wanting to give more than Rena wanted to accept; Mama didn't know my name. I couldn't work up much sympathy for Rena over her mother.

"Some people don't know how good they have things, I guess." I just said something to be responding. My mind moved on to how I was going to get out. I only agreed to go with them because Tracy wanted to go do something with her own friends and Emily wouldn't have a ride if I didn't go.

"Do you think they bought my excuse about wanting to change my clothes?" There was another problem. What was I going to change into when I got home?

"Probably," Emily answered. "But I don't see why you can't be honest and tell Rena about your mother. It isn't your fault she's like this, Clarice. You don't need to be ashamed of her. Why couldn't you just say your mother is sick and you needed to check on her?"

That wasn't exactly the lead-in I hoped for. Sometime in the next few minutes, Emily was probably going to find out my mother wore diapers and my brothers controlled my life and my father ran away and I didn't have a life. It would have been easier if she hadn't said all of that.

"I don't mean to be dishonest with anyone, Emily. I don't tell lies. I just don't throw out information that I don't need to tell. What difference does it make if she knows my mother is demented or not? Did it change your life any when you found out, or will it make any difference in a few minutes when you know that I had to come home to change my mother's diaper and put her to bed like she's a baby, and that my father ran away so he doesn't have to take care of any of us. Not that he has in a long time, anyway?"

I felt the jolt in Emily's mood clear across the car, without looking at her. That's exactly what I didn't want to happen.

She talked through a lump in her throat. "I'm so sorry, Clarice. I guess I didn't have any idea what you go through."

"Nobody does," I said. "And mostly that's how I want it to be. I don't want you to talk like this – like there's something stuck in your throat and you have to push words over it to talk to me. I don't want you to feel sorry for me because then I'll feel sorry for me too and hate what I have to do even worse than I already hate it. I feel so guilty because she can't help what happened to her and she can't help that Daddy skipped out and the boys won't change her. I don't blame them. She's their mother, for heaven's sake. They don't want to look at her that way."

"She's your mother, too, Clarice. I don't think it's natural that you have to look at her that way either. Your brothers need to grow up and your Daddy needs to be shot."

Damn, I felt tears coming and I didn't want to mess up my eyes. Especially not before David saw me. Ever since they all told me how beautiful I looked, I hoped he would be home when I got there so he could see me.

"Emily, think of what I can wear. I don't want to talk about that anymore because this is supposed to be a fun night. Help me figure out what to change into and promise me you won't pay any attention to my brothers if they act like jerks when we get there. I'm going to change my clothes, then change Mama, and leave – no matter what they say. Back that up. I'm going to change Mama first." That made her laugh a little.

"It's a deal," she promised. "Now, let's talk about Tracy's face. That ought to really get us laughing."

David said it was a definite improvement, but I shouldn't quit my day job. Michael told me I looked pretty. I took my glasses off to give them a better look, and Michael changed his opinion to *real* pretty.

"I'm going to change Mama and get her ready for bed and then I'm going out with my friends. We're supposed to meet Rena and a couple of other girls at some night club called Dancing in the Street." I said the words as fast as I could and held my breath to wait for the fireworks.

"Oh, no you aren't," David shot back. "We sat here all night while you went to the party. It's our turn to go out now. You don't have any business at Dancing in the Street in the first place. You don't know how to dance, and there's only one other reason girls go there."

"I wasn't asking your permission, David. I was telling you my plans." Emily looked like she was real proud of me for saying that and I think I saw Michael's mouth turn up a smidgeon on one side.

David huffed. "I'm leaving here in five minutes. If you leave Mama alone, it's on your conscience because it's your job to watch her at night. I tried to be nice to you, but it's like Daddy said, give a woman an inch and she'll take a mile. No more inches from me, Clarice. From here on out, I won't even try to be nice to you."

I hated that Emily was standing there taking all of this in and didn't want to make it any worse. "Emily, I'm going to change Mama. I'm sure you'd rather not see that or sit here with him, so you can wait in my room if you want."

She started toward my room, surely relieved by the offer. "Find me something to wear while I'm with Mama," I called from halfway down the hall. "I'll hurry."

Michael came back to Mama's bedroom door. "Clarice, I was going to go over to Bobby's house. Since the old man isn't here to cause a scene, I'll just ask Bobby to come over here so I can sit with Mama. You have a good time with your friends, but be careful of the guys in that place."

I appreciated Michael for saying he would watch over Mama, but was even more grateful that he thought the guys would give me a problem.

~~~

Dancing in the Street took my mind clean away from David and Mama, and most everything I ever thought about before then. I drove right up close at first, not knowing ahead of time that the parking lot filled up before nine – when we were still sitting in Rena's apartment eating the cheese ball and fruit. People walked in the middle of the street, and neon lights flashed in windows, and music blared out of the building. It put me in mind of a carnival or festival and I let go of all my problems for the time being. But nobody was dancing in the street. I hoped I would remember to ask Rena if she agreed this was another case of the wrong name for something.

I parked on a street about six blocks away, and warned Emily to lock the door when we got out of the car because I didn't know the neighborhood. I also assigned her the task of remembering where to find the car when we came back, because I knew I'd be too excited to hold on to that information once I went inside.

When I was little, the boys, and even Mama a time or two, hauled me along when they went into bars looking for Daddy. But those were rat holes around the neighborhood, where you could see the back wall from the front door, and count the customers – mostly people you already knew – on your fingers. Dancing in the Street was a real nightclub; the kind like I had only seen in movies or on TV, and I was anxious.

I understood right off why Michael warned me about the guys. Three times before we even got to the block where Dancing in the Street was located, men called out, flirting with us. One of them I knew wasn't only talking to Emily because he said ladies. Where are you pretty *ladies, pleural,* headed, to be exact.

"Should I tell him?" I asked Emily.

"No," she said almost mean like. "Just smile and keep walking."

My heart sank for a spell when we got close to the door. A huge man, who looked to me like he could earn millions of dollars if he took a notion to wrestle on TV instead of standing on the sidewalk outside of Dancing in the Street, walked up to each person in line and asked to examine their driver's license with his flashlight. He sent people packing if they didn't have a license, or didn't look like the picture on the one they had.

Even if the make-up caused him to doubt me, I figured my glasses would resolve that problem. But Emily never bothered to get her license. Without thinking, I reached over and pinched her arm. "Darn it, Em, we can't go in because you don't drive."

She massaged her arm and laughed at me. "Calm down, Girlfriend. What's come over you tonight? I have my birth certificate and my bank ID card. We'll get in."

I rubbed her arm too, feeling terrible for pinching her. "I'm so sorry. I guess excitement took over me. I can't believe I'm here, with cover girl eyelids, fixing to walk into a nightclub to hang out with my friends. Em, if I drop dead this very second, I'll die happy."

She rolled her eyes and moved my hand so I'd stop rubbing her arm. "Why do you always say that? About dying? It gives me the creeps."

"It's just a saying. I don't really put any thought behind it."

"Do me a favor and think before you say it again. I don't like to think about you dying right now, or any other time, and that's what I think every time you say that."

Emily put a damper on my excitement when she called me down that way. I turned her words over and over in my head, set upon figuring out something better to say than *if I died today* because I didn't want to make her feel sad every time something good happened to me. But our turn came up to enter Dancing in the Street before anything better came to mind, and excitement took over my thoughts again.

I stopped dead in my tracks no more than a foot inside the door. "Good Lord Almighty! I didn't know there were this many people in all of Greenville. Look at this."

Someone yelled from behind for me to get the hell out of the way. People started shoving, so Emily pulled me over to the side of the door, out of the way. I needed to stand still until my senses adjusted to Dancing in the Street. It wasn't like seeing a nightclub in a movie, or on TV where I could adjust the volume to my liking and still know it was loud in that other world on the screen. On screen, I knew the smoke and the booze stunk to high heavens, but I didn't feel it in my nose or throat. In here, I sensed the smells, and the music throbbing in my heart like the drums from the marching band when we had pep rallies in the gym.

The only one of my senses I appreciated right then was my vision. As soon as we found Rena, Jen, or Angela, I planned on putting my glasses in my purse. It was too dark to see anything anyway, so I might as well show off my cover girl eyelids.

"Watch for Angela," Emily suggested. "She'll be the easiest one to spot on account of her being so tall."

We stood beside the entrance door, on our tip toes, looking up for Angela's black hair and smooth skin to jump out of the crowd at us, never giving a thought to the possibility that she might be sitting in a chair somewhere. Two guys asked Emily to dance but we couldn't even see the dance floor from where we were so she said no thanks. One guy asked me to do something I might have to haggle over even if I was married to him. I didn't waste a no on him, I just turned my head.

"Maybe this wasn't such a great idea," I said. People pushed and insulted us and I grew weary within three minutes of getting in there. "Let's walk around once and if

125

we don't find them we can ask for our money back and leave. Maybe they already left."

Emily led the way, seeing how she was taller than me and could see better, so she got stuck meeting the troublemakers first. She pushed past most of the drunks and disrespectful people, but one old man blocked the aisle and tried to make her kiss him before he would let us pass.

She turned her back to him and looked at me square in the eye, with her lips drawn in a straight line across her face and fire in her eyes. I couldn't move because a waitress had her tray full of drinks in my back. We still hadn't spotted a familiar face but I stuck my glasses in my purse any way to protect them in case we had to fight the old man. He was still standing practically on top of Emily, breathing his liquored up breath all over her and clean past her into my face.

The waitress served the drinks on her tray and said excuse me, in a hateful tone. I thought she must hate her job to lose control that easily.

"We can't get through," I said. "That man won't let us pass on his end and you had us blocked on this side."

She pushed her way around me, caused me to bump against a table and upset two full beer bottles, and poked her tray in the old man's chest. He went sailing and landed straight on his butt since he didn't have his full balance to start with.

Emily laughed as we stepped over him, and the whole thing raised a stir when the owners of the spilled beers started fussing. I said I was sorry to them, but they said it wasn't my fault and went after the waitress.

Turned out in the end that the old guy helped us out. Rena saw him fall, from clear up on the second tier, and spotted me and Emily. That's how she knew to come rescue us and take us to the table they had up there. "That girl has some good eye sight," I said to Emily.

Dancing in the Street was fun from the second tier where we had seats and room to breathe. The music vibrated the floor, but we could talk if we yelled what we wanted to say and stuck our ear up close to hear the answer.

We had a bird's eye view of the dance floor. Rena yelled to me, "The dance most of them are doing is called swing. Looks like fun, doesn't it?" I was familiar with swing dancing from seeing it on TV, and I recognized some of the steps from the movie Grease, which I had seen about a million and one times. But I never figured on people really throwing each other around in the air like that in real life.

"It does look like fun," I yelled to Rena, "but dangerous. Do you know how to dance like that?"

"No, but Jen knows a little," she yelled back.

Jen heard her name but the whole conversation. "Jen does what?"

Rena shook her head and said we'd talk about it later. Then she jumped out of her chair and took off like a bat out of hell, chasing off to the dance floor without a partner.

Angela shrugged her shoulders and we all watched. Rena stood at the edge of the floor and waited until the song ended and the dancers filed off to sit down and catch their breath, or to look for new partners. She followed a guy to the bar and then came dragging him back to the second tier with her. When the next song came to an end, she introduced him. "This is Jansen. He's going to teach us to swing dance."

Jansen sat at our table and danced with Jen a few times, but mostly he danced with other girls who already knew the tricks. He looked like the best dancer out there to me, but my glasses were still in my purse and if I'm perfectly honest most of them looked like blurs to me from way up there.

Angela bought a bottle of wine for all of us to split. I passed since I had to drive, and because my Daddy was a drunk and my mother was demented. I wasn't aiming to turn out like either one of them.

Emily got sleepy after she drank her wine and said she was ready to leave whenever I was. I might have stayed until they closed up if she hadn't said that because I hardly gave a thought to Shady Acres while I was in Dancing in the Street.

Rena and Jansen walked us out since we had so much trouble walking through the first time. They teased us about that most of the night, and called us troublemakers.

The should-have-been-a-wrestler guy sat on a stool because there wasn't anybody left in line for him to investigate. He said goodnight and come back, and I said I would. Emily ignored him.

Rena picked up on her mother's habit and hugged us and said thanks for coming and stuff like that, like this was her house. I guessed since we started at her apartment, she thought she was still responsible for acting like a hostess. Jansen jumped in like he was afraid of being left out. He hugged Emily first, and then me, and I thought he hugged me a little bit longer.

"Rena has my phone number," he said. "Call when you get ready for dance lessons."

"Are you serious?" I got excited all over again and hoped I'd calm down enough to remember to put my glasses on before I started driving. I was about to get used to being blind and deaf. "I do want to learn. It looks like fun."

Rena agreed. "Jansen can come to my apartment and teach us all together. If that's okay with everyone."

"I would enjoy that," he said. "I had fun with you girls tonight. Have you known each other long?"

"Not really." I smiled at Rena, feeling like we were truly friends after the makeover and Dancing in the Street. "It's a funny thing how it all happened. I guess opposites really do attract.

Chapter 16

I held my stamped hand under the black light to verify legitimacy for readmission, and secured a pompous nod from the neckless hulk whose sole credential was size. Jansen, my volunteer bodyguard, trailed close, talking about something I hoped was unimportant since I had nearly forgotten he was there. Although Jansen exceeded the prerequisites for his vacuum cleaner sales position, his baby face and delicate frame left doubt that he could more than scream if confronted by the likes of the hulk.

We returned to our seats on the upper level, where Jen's cousin and a friend had filled the seats Emily and Clarice vacated. Jansen huddled over the tiny round table and tried to shout his way into the conversation. I withdrew into my own world, which felt slightly less comfortable than the harsh atmosphere of blaring music, flashing lights, drunken voices, and stale air that I was escaping.

Jan switched seats when Jansen and the cousin organized a search party and left to find our missing waitress, and started a probe of her own.

"You look like you lost your best friend. Are you okay?"

I pressed on her arm. "I think you're still here. I must be okay."

"Funny, Rena. If you're worried about the waitress, I'm sure they'll find her. Cheer up."

"I'm tired," I lied. "My domestic efforts caught up with me."

She told me again how successful my makeovers – both cosmetic and domestic – had been, and said she understood how tired I must be after all that work.

"If you don't mind, I think I'll head out and get some sleep."

The guys came back with a new server. Jansen ordered a drink, left money on the table to cover it, and offered to walk me out.

"She's the luckiest person I know when it comes to parking," Jen told him. "She's in the lot, right outside the door."

"I had to be lucky at something, and parking isn't too much to ask." I turned from Jen to Jansen. "She's jealous. I took the last space. The assistant pulled out the 'lot full' sign and turned Jen away. I'll be fine alone, Jansen, sit down and enjoy your drink."

I wanted to be alone, but Jansen insisted that he didn't mind and the look on his face told me he would be crushed if I rejected his chivalry. I said goodnight to everyone else and walked out with Jansen a step behind.

This time through, the first floor was less crowded, but the people who remained were twice as obnoxious as they had been earlier. The ones who weren't a drink away from comatose were either looking for a fight or searching desperately to find someone to pair up with before closing time. I didn't understand what attracted Jen to Dancing in the Street.

Since neither Jansen nor I looked like we wanted to fight or pair up, we sailed straight through, out the door and past the hulk with no problem. I welcomed the blast of cool night air – or morning air for my dad and the paperboy – that smacked me in the face. A hollow, fuzzy feeling in my head replaced the loud music, but brought me back to the reality that I had numbly been avoiding. Tears stung my eyes and I tried to blink them away so Jansen wouldn't notice.

"I'm glad you remembered me and came up to speak," he said. "I had a good time with you and your friends." I nodded. After an uncomfortable space of silence, he continued. "You seemed to have a great time together. What were you guys celebrating tonight?"

"We weren't celebrating. It was just a ladies' night out."

"I guess I sort of blew that then, I apologize."

I stopped beside my car. "No need. I invited you to join us. Actually tracked you down and practically insisted." I pointed to the car, unable to stop the tears. "Here I am."

"Is something wrong? You've been quiet since we went back in earlier. I'm a good listener if you want to talk about it."

I wanted to lie and say nothing was wrong, jump in my car as quickly as possible, and get out of there. But I sensed he probably was a good listener, and my tears apparently wanted me to share them with him since they showed no sign of stopping.

Unlike Rodrigo, Jansen stayed put in the passenger seat of my car instead of jumping in and out. He also listened to me talk about myself instead of telling me his life story. And no one interrupted us, not even the patrons from Dancing in the Street who continued to look for someone to pair up with in the parking lot.

"The whole thing is really very childish and I can't believe I am reacting this way. I'm confused about something Clarice said to you. Actually, I'm hurt more than confused and I'm sort of embarrassed to tell you."

"I can't help if you don't tell me," he said. "I doubt she meant to hurt you. What was it?"

"Opposites attract."

His smile encouraged me to continue although I knew he couldn't possibly understand.

"I know Clarice didn't intend to hurt my feelings. She is the kindest person I have ever known. She's kind, she's gentle, she's generous, and she's levelheaded. She's dependable and proud. She wouldn't hurt anyone."

"Clarice is the little one with spikey hair?"

"Right. And the beautiful eyes. That's Clarice."

He studied me closely. "I don't know either of you, really. But I'd say most people would look at the two of you and guess you are opposites. From what I saw tonight, you are more outgoing and stress-free. But, like I said, I don't really know you."

"I think this was the first time she has ever been out to a place like Dancing in the Street," I explained.

"Why are you upset?"

"Think about it Jansen. If she's all of the things I just told you she is, and I'm the opposite, what does that make me? Unkind, harsh, selfish, a scatter-brain?"

He lowered his head with a grimace. What had I said that could have wounded him? Being with me probably was enough. He probably wished he had left with the simple disappointments that I knew nothing about vacuum cleaners and I couldn't dance.

"I could keep you awake all night with my problems. This is silly, and I'll be embarrassed in the morning when I think about how crazy I must sound to you. I'll let you go home and get to sleep now if you promise you'll forget all of this."

"Are you this hard on everyone," he asked, "or just yourself?"

I laughed and wanted to skip the question, but he looked to me for an answer. "Neither. I'm even harder on my mother. If you have about a week, I'll tell you about that problem too. I reserve my abusive behavior to the two of us though, no one else."

Jansen didn't relinquish his next week to hear about Mother. "Your limit is one problem a night. Back to Clarice and the opposites. I'll bet she didn't mean it the way you took it. Call her in the morning and clear it up. She seems like a nice girl."

"She is." I answered too quickly and worried that he would suspect my matchmaking intentions. "That's the problem. She's nice and I'm the opposite. Remember?"

Jansen rested his head back against the seat and closed his eyes. "I'm not sleeping. I'm thinking," he said.

How's this – there are different ways to be opposite. It isn't always bad."

I couldn't believe he dissected words. He was going to fit in perfectly with Clarice and me. "Remind me on a night when I haven't introduced another problem to ask your opinion of sweater versus warmer."

"That should be interesting. Think about this, Rena. Here's two people being nice in different ways. Person one goes out of her way to invite the other to do fun things. She plans a big make-up party to boost someone's self-esteem. That was nice. The other would never do anything like that, but she's full of inspiration and love. There – he looked proud of himself – we have two people who are nice in opposite ways. Sort of."

"Why are you selling vacuum cleaners, Jansen? You should be charging one forty an hour to listen to insanity and regurgitate it in rational terms. Who told you about the makeover?"

"Clarice did. She loves you for it. She didn't say it in those words, because I have a feeling those are words Clarice is afraid to use. But I read between the lines. Are you planning the dance lessons for the same reason?"

"Phantom pain." It was a whisper but he heard, and he looked at me like I had lost what little I had left of my mind. "I'm having phantom pain." I couldn't look at him anymore. *I* worried that I was losing my mind, so he was bound to have come to the same conclusion. Or read it between my lines.

Jansen stretched his arm across the car, first to hold on to the headrest and test the water I guess, before he massaged the back of my neck. Physically it was comforting. Emotionally, I splintered.

I felt like a traitor – to Clarice because I pictured her with Jansen, not me – to Jansen because I pulled him into my life without defining his role or my intentions – and to myself because I didn't want him to take his hand away and this wasn't what I had planned at all.

But worse than feeling like a traitor, I felt like an opposite. Clarice would never put herself in the position I was in.

Headlights divided surgeons and paperboys from party animals and armchair shrinks; those headed toward home still had theirs burning and those on their way out didn't see the need. I used my headlights to drive home from Dancing in the Street and, thanks to the cotton curtains guarding the slits in my blinds, needed to turn on a light to see my way into the apartment.

A quick glimpse of the food trays and dirty glasses on the table ousted my desire for light. I flipped the switch and dove for the couch, where I closed my eyes to lay with my legs curled and last night's make-up seeping into my pores.

Jansen was right. I should call Clarice and clear this up. She would call me girlfriend and say no offense intended, and I would feel like the idiot that I was, only a much-relieved idiot so it would be worth the embarrassment.

Jansen was also right to take his hand away and stay on his own side of the car when he realized his massage wasn't totally comforting.

I made up my mind to sleep until my head cleared and I could focus my eyes to read the phone book. Hopefully, she'd be listed.

I woke with a stiff neck, a headache, and a heavy heart, partly because there were six worthless make-up mirrors--that I would eventually have to pay for--stacked in boxes beside my table. Mostly, however, I felt sad because I was obsessed with believing that I was an opposite of Clarice. Eight hours of sleep and the full light of day reinforced the pain instead of easing it like Janson promised.

I considered the likelihood that this was my retribution for the pain I had inflicted on Clarice with my *generic* response, hoping I had come to a pivotal point where I could resolve both issues and put them behind me. Clarice deserved a full explanation including the reasons and emotions that prompted the word generic as my response to her question. Then, she might offer the same to me regarding her opposites attract statement.

With effort, I unfolded my legs and rolled into a sitting position, supporting my neck with both hands. Half of the day was already gone and it looked like I would lose another hour or so pulling myself together.

Inching my way to the bathroom, I tried to remember where I had stuffed the phone book during my frantic cleaning spree. Under my bed or on the closet floor seemed the most likely possibilities, and they both required bending over, so the phone call had to wait until after my shower.

I smeared cleansing cream on my face, using my ring finger around the eyes as Angela instructed, and swallowed two Tylenols before stepping into the hot water. Once I found the perfect position with the water hitting the sore spot on my neck, the pain eased and I believed there was hope for the day.

There was a whole column of McDaniels listings in the phone book, none of them for Clarice McDaniels since she lived with her parents. The second one I dialed was the one I needed. A male answered, probably a brother I thought because he sounded too young to be her father.

"She ain't here. She should be down at the Laundromat, but Cinderella went shopping with somebody named Charlotte instead."

Chapter 17

"Michael, please, I'm begging you from the bottom of my heart." I was fixing to fold my hands and drop to my knees if all else failed. "I can't let this chance pass over me."

"Clarice, trotting off to parties and dance clubs is one thing. This is another story. The McDaniels don't accept charity."

"I told you, it isn't charity. It's a lucky break. Nobody said we can't take a lucky break if it pops up, did they?"

He eased up on his frown which made me glad. I didn't want to have to drop to my knees and I knew I had already pushed my luck with telling instead of asking.

I decided to try one more time to explain the lucky break. "One Stop EyeCare is offering a special deal. If you buy contact lenses, you get a free pair of glasses to go with them. Charlotte only wears her glasses part time, when she's reading notes in court mostly, so she doesn't need the contact lenses. If we go in together, I can get the contacts and she'll get the glasses. Since I wasn't aiming to get anything in the first place and she was, it's fair that she wants to pay. I'm not taking charity from her if it doesn't cost her anything."

"It sounds like charity to me," Michael insisted. "You have what you need. You have glasses. Why can't you ever be satisfied?"

"My glasses are a joke and you know it, Michael. These were Mama's old frames. We just took them over to Ward Optical and they changed the lenses to my prescription. Come on. Remember how good I looked with my make-up on? You said I was real pretty when I took my glasses off. I want to look like that all the time. Please."

"I guess I can't stop you if this is what you want to do," he said. "What does this have to do with me going to the Laundromat?"

"Mama's in her last gown. I'm not asking you to do everything. Just one load of her gowns and under things so if she has an accident while I'm gone I'll be able to change her before I go out to do the rest of the laundry. Please, Michael. I'm begging you."

I wasted half the morning begging the nicer of my two brothers before he gave in and agreed to help. Then, he had to convince David to stay with Mama while he went to the Laundromat. He used the excuse of helping me not look so ugly again, and it worked, again. I didn't much care anymore. They could make fun of me all they wanted so long as I got out.

Charlotte offered to pick me up in her car. That would be charity, since it was clear on the opposite end of town and out of her way. But it didn't cross my mind to say yes in the first place. I wouldn't let her come anywhere near Shady Acres on any account.

I wanted to hang around in the living room and talk to Michael. I believed he wanted to make up to me, maybe even be my friend. When Daddy left, Michael let go of most of his anger as far as I could see, and he finally noticed I was a real person, not a little girl to tease. I wanted to ask about his job on the barge, and ask when he was fixing to leave. But I needed to use what little time I had left after begging to fix Mama's lunch and get myself ready.

David picked up the anger Michael let go and acted more like Daddy every day. He pitched a fit over me going to One Stop EyeCare with Charlotte Boiles and tried to stand between me and the door so I couldn't leave. I stood there with my hand on my hip, looking as much like Mama before she skipped out on us as he looked like Daddy, except I was about a hundred pounds lighter than Mama.

"I aim to go whether you want me to or not, so you may as well move out of my way before you get Mama going. She's quiet now and might sleep while I'm gone if you don't upset her." Inside, my stomach tied up in knots, but I never let on where he could see I was upset. "The way I see it, David, I'm the boss of this house until you grow up enough to pay the bills. Even then, you won't have control over me. If you don't move out of my way, I might take a notion not to ever come back once I get out."

David turned to Michael for help but didn't get any. "She's getting a little big for her britches, don't you think?"

Michael told him to move away from the door.

One Step EyeCare wasn't as crowded as I pictured it to be, especially considering the deal they offered. The parking lot was half empty.

Charlotte waited by the door so I didn't have to hunt for her when I got inside. She looked like a lawyer, dressed in a navy blue suit and white blouse, which seemed strange with it being Saturday and all. I think she looked even prettier dressed that way than she had in her fancy party clothes.

She smiled when she caught sight of me. I thought about how my mother used to smile when I came in from school. It made me glad to be home, no matter how many of those savages laughed when the bus let me out at the entrance to Shady Acres. Mama said not to pay them any mind. Anybody left on the bus when I got off had to live in Conway Heights, and those houses were nothing more than trailers without wheels. She told me to pity them for their ignorance.

I smiled back at Charlotte, deciding it would be rude to tell her I liked her better in her lawyer clothes. She looked more like a mother that way, and I didn't think that was to her liking.

"I went ahead and registered us," Charlotte said. "That should reduce our waiting time by a few minutes." She led me around the corner to a large waiting room filled with plastic and chrome chairs. Most of them were empty.

"I'll bet somebody's goose gets cooked for not advertising this sale better," I said. "There's hardly anybody here."

Charlotte smiled and nodded. "It's unfortunate for business, but works to our advantage. The wait will be short."

That made twice she brought up waiting time, so I figured she wore the suit because she had an appointment. "If something came up and this isn't a good day for you, we can leave," I offered. "I'm sure they'll run the sale again some time."

I had my heart set on the contacts now that I came so near to getting them, but I could live without them if need be. Charlotte calmed me down right away. Her schedule was free, she just hated to be kept waiting. When the girl called my name to go back first, I told Charlotte to go before me to ease her tension. While we still argued back and forth over it, they called her name too.

All in all, the whole process didn't take near as long as I thought it would. One Stop was good for its name because they did everything while we waited – examined our eyes and made our contacts and glasses.

They put us in separate examination rooms so we could both see doctors at the same time. The contact examination took longer because they had to do special measurements, so Charlotte waited for me in a chair outside the door to my room. From there, we went over to the glasses shop, still in the same building.

There must have been a million and one choices, some of them so expensive they were locked up in special cases like the cameras at K-Mart. I figured on Charlotte heading directly to the designer counter to try on some locked-up frames, but she didn't. She picked up practically the first glasses she saw and ordered them. I put more thought into picking out a new toothbrush.

The people in contacts gave me a scare at first. Because they didn't seem to be in a hurry about anything, I figured Charlotte would be disappointed about wasted time and fixing to tell me we needed to leave. But she surprised me. She followed me through the different stations, and watched me poke my fingers in my eyes while I learned to put my contacts in and take them back out. She laughed at me some times, in a nice way, and told me I would get used to it. And when I had them in and looked at myself in the mirror, she told me I was beautiful, even without my make-up.

The lady at One Stop EyeCare gave me a schedule to follow so I could gradually get used to wearing the contacts. She advised me to take them out for the drive home and then put them back in when I got home. I wanted to walk in the door and surprise Michael, but I took her advice and waited.

The surprise was on me when I got home. I heard David and Michael fighting before I got out of the car, and as soon as I opened the door to the trailer I heard Mama doing her part in the bedroom.

"How fucking stupid are you?" David asked Michael. "You don't know by now that you can't turn your back on anything around here?"

He turned his anger on me as soon as I walked in. "It's all your fault, Cinderella, having to run around instead of sticking to your responsibilities around here."

"What's my fault? Is Mama okay?" My heart pounded, thinking they let something happen to her while I was gone.

"She's okay, but she'll be naked from here on out. Dumbass left her clothes in the washer and went over to Grayson's Pub to shoot darts while they washed. Somebody made off with the clothes while he was gone."

I felt sorry for Michael, but David was right. He should have known better than to do that. "Everything she owned was in that load, Michael, she won't have anything left to wear." After I thought about it, I felt sorry for anybody desperate enough to want Mama's raggedly old gowns and stained up undies.

"You'll just have to pull some money out of your Cinderella account and buy her something," David ordered. "You should have been here doing the laundry yourself instead of dumping it on Michael."

I went back to check and make sure she hadn't messed up the gown she was wearing. The gown was dry and I changed her diaper to make sure she stayed that way.

"I don't figure this is all my fault," I told my brothers. "I see equal blame on me and Michael, since I left him to do my job and he messed it up. But Mama is equally your responsibility, David. I think we all need to pitch in to buy her new clothes. How much do you have?"

They denied having any money but I knew as sure as I was standing there they could both pull out enough to buy a beer if they wanted.

I picked up my purse and told them to watch her while I was gone. Michael promised he'd pay me back when he got his first check from the barge. I walked past them without saying anything, and slammed the door on my way out so she'd holler the whole time I was gone.

By the time I got back with three new gowns and five pairs of underwear, I wasn't much in the mood to show off my new contacts. I put them in and sat on my bed getting used to them where nobody could see me.

Chapter 18

Dad sat through my flat recap of the makeover, but my best attempt at theatrics did little to distract his attention from the ottoman he apparently found more interesting than my reason for being there. My self-esteem suffered when both parents shunned me on the same day.

"And then, with no warning or lead-in whatsoever, Mother jumped up from her chair and announced her pregnancy," I said.

That drew him away from the ottoman. "She did what?"

"I'm just checking to see if you're listening to anything I'm saying. It looks like you aren't any more interested in makeovers than I am."

"Sorry," he said. "My mind was somewhere else."

"The good news is, I have clean pores and the apartment looks great."

"Your mother told me."

It was my turn to be shocked. "She did what?"

"She said you finally hung curtains and they look nice. And she complimented you for organizing the get together. Said you went *all out*."

That left me speechless because the only thing I could think to ask was had she told him my bedroom was still a disaster. If she hadn't, I didn't want to expose that truth myself. If she had, I would stop worrying about her.

"Why are you here, Rena? You know I'm always happy to see you, but I don't believe you dropped by to chat about the makeup party or your clean apartment any more than I believe you called me early one morning because you wanted to reminisce about an old birthday party."

I turned my eyes to the ottoman, hoping it might give me an answer to the question it had given him.

"If something is bothering you, Rena, you can tell me. I can't read your mind or make any sense of your rambling around issues. So, if you want my help you need to spell it out for me."

"Did she take Clarice shopping? Is that where she is?"

"Do you have some objection to your mother spending time with your friend? I remember a time – not too very long ago, actually – when you complained that she didn't like any of your friends."

"They didn't invite me, Dad." I knew that had to be Mother's idea. Clarice wouldn't have left me out. "Mother has plenty of friends. Why would she suddenly want to shop with mine? Dad, the problem is that she's trying to change Clarice. She probably has her in Larry's clinic right now and we'll never recognize her again. Why can't she let people be who they want to be?"

"Clarice called here this morning. I answered the phone and she sounded quite cheerful. I don't believe you need to worry that your mother took her anywhere against her will."

"Mother told her to call. Clarice is too polite not to comply. Crap! I don't want to talk about this." I picked my purse up from the floor. "I'm going home to stew over this alone. I have a mess to clean up."

He took his eyes off the ottoman and looked up at me. "Would that be the mess left after your attempt to impress and change Clarice?"

"That isn't fair, Dad. I wasn't trying to change her."

He kept his eyes on me. "I see. So you decided you wanted to spruce up and you needed the help of Clarice and her friends to do it?"

"No. I planned that stupid party because I wanted to be fair, to Clarice and to Mother. I wanted to find out if Clarice was unhappy with her appearance before I continued criticizing Mother too harshly for jumping to that conclusion."

"Did you find your answer? Did Clarice enjoy your makeover and show an interest in working on her appearance?"

I flopped back down on the couch with a sigh. "Yes."

"So what's the problem now?"

Mother's garage door opened and her Mercedes pulled in. I heard her shut off the engine and get out of the car, relieved when I didn't hear a second door open and close. I wasn't ready to face Clarice.

Maybe I was the one jumping to conclusions; Mother was dressed for work. I imagined Dad was gloating over his clever scam. I tried to think of some way to get back at him while I watched his face for the smile that would give him away. He was focused on the ottoman again without a hint of a smile.

Mother spoke, and then he smiled. "Hi, Rena. This is a nice surprise."

She hung her jacket over the back of the desk chair and kicked her shoes under it. Then. She came to sit beside me on the couch, closer than I wanted her to be. "I have a surprise for you as well."

"Let me guess," I interrupted. "You took Clarice out and told her how hopeless she looked, so she let you change everything about her?"

I hated myself when I saw her face melt.

"Not at all, Rena. I went with Clarice this morning to be with her while she learned to insert and remove her new contact lenses. I would have thought you'd be happy for her."

I nodded.

"And Rena, I didn't tell her she was hopeless. I believe I'm the one who made over her last night, and told her she had beautiful eyes before the make-up. She told me she wanted contacts. I didn't suggest them."

I said I was sorry for being so cruel to my mother and meant it. "Please, tell me you didn't insult her pride by paying for them."

"I didn't insult her by paying for them. I found out last night that you were correct when you said she's too proud to accept help. I offered to help with her cosmetic purchase and she wouldn't allow it. You have my word that I won't insult her, Rena."

"How did she do with the lenses?" Dad asked, but it should have been my question.

"She did very well," Mother reported. "She got so excited. It was actually very refreshing to watch her. She was like a little girl in her excitement, and she was so appreciative of something that most people take for granted. Rena, I like your new friend."

"I like her too," I said, noting that *new* was a definite improvement over *poor little*.

Dad threw in his contribution. "Charlotte, did you offer to help Rena with her purchases? From what you've told me, it sounds like this was an expensive party."

I wanted to melt into the couch and disappear. "Dad, do you honestly think I'm jealous of the attention Mother showed Clarice? I don't want Mother's money, and I don't begrudge anyone she chooses to spend it on or give it to. Don't either of you understand that I'm only trying to protect my friend?"

Mother said she believed she did understand.

That was a start.

~~~

Clarice must have been on pins and needles watching for me to come in Monday morning. She knocked on her window the instant I came through the outer door. With her face almost touching the glass, she pointed to her eyes and fluttered her lids dramatically. She glowed, and wore the widest smile I had ever seen on her face.

I understood immediately what Mother had seen in Clarice when she witnessed the contact lens fitting. Clarice projected the incredible exuberance that a child possesses before disappointments in life induce inhibitions. Perfect innocence. Seeing that in an adult was more than a bit overwhelming.

The contrast between this side of Clarice and the strong, wise person I had learned to depend on for strength was endearing. I wanted to meet the parents who successfully sheltered her through twenty-three years of this harsh world without letting any of the ugliness get close to her. Like them, I wanted to build a wall around Clarice and protect her from anything that might spoil her naiveté.

Maybe that was how Mother felt when I walked in the house that day, painted like a streetwalker in Jen's sister's black eyeliner. Mother's reaction finally made sense to me now that I had seen Clarice in her contacts.

I waved at her through the window and rushed past the three empty windows that had been closed since I came to work at GWS - and would stay that was as long as Clarice took up the slack without complaining - and entered the door that transformed me from public to employee.

She turned to face me. "What do you think, Rena? No glasses." She giggled with excitement, every fiber of her body screaming *I feel beautiful.*

"I think you look great." I tried to match her enthusiasm without sounding as phony as Mother's plastic friends. "How do they feel? Does it hurt?"

"Other than feeling weird to purposely stick something in my eyes after spending my whole life trying to keep everything out of them, they don't hurt at all. I still have to work up on a schedule this week and adjust. I'll be up to full time when my eye make-up comes in, so I won't have to worry about smearing it up when I take them in and out. Oh, Rena, everything is working out perfect."

She wiped her mouth – grinned from ear to ear – and wiped again. "I can't drive in them yet, so I didn't see outside. But everything in here looks good."

Her shoulders shook in something that looked like a combination shiver and shimmy. "No more glasses, Girlfriend. I'm so excited!"

"I'm excited for you Clarice." That was true in the same sense that I was happy for Jen when she beat me in tennis. Happy for her but sad for me at the same time. I enjoyed seeing Clarice this excited but strangely and selfishly felt empty. I loved her the way she was and feared I would lose my rock (my word and it surprised me to realize that's how I had come to look at her) a piece at a time.

Clarice blinked often while she took care of her customers that morning; whether out of necessity or so they would notice her contacts, I wasn't sure. She removed the lenses for a thirty minute rest mid-morning and said it was easier to get them back in each time.

"I think I'm a natural at this, Rena. I'm so grateful for the good luck of your Mama needing to get new glasses during the special. Do you think that's an evil thought on my part? I appreciate her, too, for even thinking to take me."

I almost ruined everything. Mother didn't need glasses and I came close to blurting that out without thinking.

"Mother replaced her glasses?" I needed clarification. "I didn't realize she needed to do that."

"Yes. She left hers behind in a courtroom on Friday and when she went back after them just a few minutes later, they were already gone. Seems to me like the city ought to have some kind of insurance to cover losses like that, but your mama wanted to run on over to One Stop EyeCare and get a new pair made real fast on Saturday so she'd have them in court today."

"And they had a special?" I prompted.

"Buy one, get one free. One pair of contacts and one pair of glasses go together for the special. Your mama didn't need the contacts and didn't want to see the special go to waste, so she offered me the free contacts half. I'm so grateful. Your mother really is nice, Rena."

"Yes, she is." Nicer than I realized, and much nicer than Clarice could imagine, or than I could or wanted to tell her.

Mother drove past a One Stop EyeCare location with me in her car once. She carried on for miles about how she would rather be blind than have a bunch of half-trained technicians herd her through stations like an animal going down for the slaughter. Had she really sacrificed her Saturday to be herded through One Stop EyeCare for glasses she didn't need so Clarice could have the free contacts? Was my world really turning upside down?

Maybe she did need glasses. She passed forty a few years back but wouldn't let any of us acknowledge that fact. She swore she'd never speak to anyone who sent her black balloons or put a tacky Lordy Lordy looks who's forty sign in the yard. And we believed her. But she would never choose One Stop. I knew the truth.

I hung Clarice's closed sign on her window five minutes before lunchtime because there were no customers in line.

"Go put the drops in your eyes or do whatever it is you need to do," I ordered. "You're about to see the outside world through contact lenses."

She jumped down off her stool with a smile and went to get her purse from the filing cabinet. I answered her line when it rang so she could go to the ladies' room and take care of her drops.

"Clarice you have to come home." It was a male voice, in an obvious panic.

"This is Rena," I said. "Hold on and I'll get Clarice."

"Just tell her Mama fell out of bed and she has to come home."

I heard screaming in the background. A woman's voice, obviously in agonizing pain, for a brief moment before he hung up.

"Don't close the drawer," I called over my shoulder to Clarice. "I need to get my purse."

I hung my closed sign and ran to Ann's office to tell her what had happened, and that I was driving Clarice home.

Chapter 19

Clarice plunged from on top of the world to deep despair when I told her about the phone call. If I could have taken care of the problem without telling her about it, I would have, but it wasn't possible. The most I could do was offer to drive her home and stay with her while she went through whatever was in store for her.

"I can drive my own car," she insisted. "You go on to lunch and I'll let you know what's going on when you get back."

I followed her through the building and down the block to the employee parking lot, keeping step with her irregular pace, repeating the same conversation several times.

In a rush of quick steps, I said, "Clarice you are in no condition to drive."

She stopped dead in her tracks to answer. "I'm fine.

We took a few more quick steps while I said, "You're upset. I want to go with you."

She stopped again to say, "No offense, but I'll be fine without you."

After a few rounds, it was obvious that I was getting nowhere, so I tried a new approach. "You aren't supposed to drive with your contacts in yet."

"The doctor didn't actually say that," she said. "I'm not restricted."

I reminded her that she hadn't felt comfortable enough to wear them when she drove to work a few hours earlier. "I won't let you drive, Clarice. That's final."

I coaxed her into my car, but she let me know it was still under protest, even though she had given up forcing me to repeat the argument. By that time, she was crying and worried that she probably should remove her contacts. But she didn't' think she could do that in the car.

"Clarice, you have to direct me," I said when I stopped the car at the parking lot exit. "I don't know where you live."

Light sobs accompanied her tears. She didn't respond until another car pulled up behind mine and the driver tapped lightly on the horn.

"Turn left." Now she was sobbing.

I drove slowly, waiting for further directions, and waved at the patient co-worker who pulled his car around us once we were on the road. "Let's try to think positively, Clarice. I want to believe your mother's injuries will be minimal when we get there. Has she been sick long?"

"About five years," she said, sounding unsure of her answer. "It's hard to keep track after a while. She was still pretty good when I was in high school, but started feeling bad the summer after I graduated. That's why I went ahead and took a job instead of going on to college."

"I'm sorry to hear that," I told her. "Sorry you didn't get to finish school, and very sorry that your mother has been sick for so long."

Clarice sniffed and let out a mournful sigh. "I reckon I have to get this over with sooner than later now. Rena, I live in Shady Acres trailer park off Highway 24. If you don't want to drive clean out there, you can let me out at the next corner and I'll catch the bus. I won't drive, I promise."

She turned her face toward the window on her side of the car, refusing to look back at me. A huge piece of her heart came out in those words and I wanted to sob with her. There went another piece of my friend.

I hurt, not because she lived in Shady Acres, but because people had made her so ashamed that she kept it hidden. But I realized quickly that I had no right to pretend that I was any different from those who had made her feel ashamed since the next thought that entered my mind was that I would never have guessed Clarice came from that environment. My preconceived ideas were just as harmful as the people I was criticizing. Clarice must have known that about me or she would have told me where she lived long before an emergency forced the issue.

Maybe I really was an opposite.

"I'm taking you home, Clarice, and I want to stay with you while you help your mother. Listen, Girlfriend, we're in this together."

She continued to stare out the window, sniffing occasionally although it seemed to be slowing. I turned onto Lincoln Lane and headed south toward Highway 24.

"No offense, Girlfriend, but you shouldn't call me girlfriend. You sounded like somebody's mother trying to make like she's young. But thanks."

We both laughed. "I felt like I was trying to speak a foreign language," I admitted. "At least I made you talk to me again. I even got a laugh out of you."

"I didn't tell you everything you need to know if you're really aiming to come in with me when we get there," she warned. "You need to be prepared."

"Then start preparing me, because I intend to stay with you."

She took a deep breath and exhaled it slowly. "My mother isn't in her right mind. She has dementia. My father skipped out shortly after your barbecue and we haven't seen hide nor hair of him since, which sets fine with me because his brain is half ate up with alcohol."

I had no response; it was more than I could process in the few seconds it took to hear it.

"At least Mama and Daddy have semi-legitimate excuses. My brothers, well at least my brother David, is just a mean worthless blob of flesh that doesn't deserve the air it breathes. Michael at least tries to be nice at times. Rena, I apologize right now in advance of getting there because they'll surely embarrass me."

I did have a response to that. "Clarice, you don't need to apologize for your family. You don't control them do you?"

"Mercy, no," she answered. "If I had any control over them things would be a whole lot different. They'd have jobs for one thing."

"Your brothers don't work? How old are they?"

"They're both older than me. David's the oldest. He's twenty-seven. Michael's thirteen months younger than him, but seems a heap older in maturity. He's fixing to go to work on the barges as soon as they come back in."

It was truly more than I could comprehend, so I returned to a topic that felt somewhat safe. "Has your mother fallen before?"

"She slipped once when I was helping her out of the bath tub. After that I wouldn't put her in there anymore unless somebody else was home. Not that having the boys around makes much difference. They won't look at her – you know – doing private things like taking a bath. Rena, she hasn't had a bath since Daddy ran off. I wash her in the bed."

I felt sick at my stomach thinking about Clarice bathing her demented mother in her bed. No wonder she spent as much time as possible at GWS. She never gave any indication that she lived this unnatural, pitiful life. Earlier that very day I thought she must have remarkably wonderful parents to have sheltered her. Now, I saw that she protected herself. The contract lenses probably *were* the most exciting thing that had happened to her in a long time.

"How are your eyes holding up?"

"I think they're okay. Things look a little blurry, probably because I cried on them."

Clarice pointed to a wooden sign ahead. "There's Shady Acres. Don't bother looking for the shade. We can talk about the name later."

She pointed out the small brown and white aluminum home that was probably older than she was, and said I could park on the gravel plot in front. Before she opened the car door to run inside, she squeezed my hand and thanked me.

I walked into the trailer a few steps behind Clarice. As far as I could remember that was the first time I had been inside a mobile home. Under different circumstances I probably would have been pleasantly surprised at how much like a real house it seemed once I got inside. But these weren't normal circumstances so all I could think about was the screaming woman Clarice called Mama. She lay on the bed, so the brothers at least had picked her up off the floor and helped her back in.

"I'm sorry David called you," the smaller brother said. "Mama's fine. You all can go back to work."

"I'm Rena," I said, unsure whether to offer my hand for a shake.

"Yeah, she talks about you. I'm Michael, Clarice's brother."

I didn't tell him she tried not to talk about him. "Are you sure your mother is okay? She's screaming." The sound was making me sick at my stomach again.

"She hollers like that pretty much all the time," he told me. "It don't sound no different to me so I think she's just mad about falling. She don't look hurt."

Clarice's voice mingled with the screaming. "Why'd you move her, David? What if she broke a bone or something? You might have made it worse."

"Hey, Cinderella, if you don't like the way we do things you can stay here and take care of her yourself. I don't need you criticizing every move I make," was the response, I assumed from David.

"Does she have a doctor?" I asked Michael, remembering he was the nice one. "Perhaps she should be seen by a doctor to rule out injuries."

"She used to have one, but he quit her when Dad refused to let him bleed us dry over the dementia diagnosis. Nothing's going to help her, but Doc Shuber wanted Dad to parade her all over town to specialists and he knew she didn't have any insurance."

I managed a smile that I hoped he would accept as a positive response, as well as an ending to the conversation.

"Can I see her?" I didn't want to see the mother, really, but I wanted to talk to Clarice.

"Be my guest," he said. "End of the hall." He butted his head in the direction of the opening on the other side of the kitchen, as though I couldn't already see the room from where I stood.

I walked down the narrow paneled space that served as a hall, thinking that was the most inappropriate use of terminology yet, and stopped in the doorframe of the room where Clarice stood examining her mother's body for injuries. The screaming seemed to have lessened in severity since Clarice entered the room.

"Is she hurt," I asked, self-consciously doubting my decision to intrude.

Clarice shrugged. "I can't find anything wrong, but how can I be sure?"

David walked toward the door where I stood so I stepped inside the room to allow him room to pass.

"Clarice," I asked, "do you want me to call Dad? He's a doctor. At least he can tell us what to look for, or what to do."

I expected to find a petite woman in the bed, because Clarice was so small herself, and because she had spoken of helping her mother in and out of the bathtub. I nearly gasped when I saw that the mother easily weighed over two hundred pounds.

"I don't know what to do," she answered. "Mama doesn't have insurance, but I can't leave her here not knowing if she's hurt."

She tried to get through to the woman. "Mama, can you hear me? This is my friend, Rena, the one who invited me to the barbecue and the make-up party. Can you see her, Mama?"

I smiled, although the woman gave no indication that she had heard anything her daughter said, or that she saw me standing at the foot of her bed. She continued to yell sounds that fell short of forming words or expressing emotions. I wasn't convinced that they were cries of pain.

"I think you need some layers around your face," Clarice said.

Had she lost her mind, too? My expression must have asked the question for me.

"Your hair," she said. "It just came to me. That's what we should do with your hair. It will add volume, soften your face, and it won't be hard to fix in the morning since you can't seem to get up on time."

"That sounds good to me," I told her. "You can take care of my hair as soon as we get your mother's problems under control. Want me to call Dad?"

Tears filled Clarice's eyes and she nodded.

Dad was in surgery, so I explained the situation and left a message with the operating room schedule coordinator at St. Mark's Community Hospital.

"I'd be happy to take the message for you, but I think it would be best to call an ambulance," the coordinator suggested. "She may have fractured something that you can't see. Is she responsive? Can she tell you where she hurts?"

"She's responsive, and the answer to your second question is no." I hoped she wouldn't force me to explain in front of Clarice.

"You really should call an ambulance. I'll alert your father that you'll be coming to the emergency room if you want."

I said I would, and she could, and thank you, knowing Clarice would be relieved to get help for her mother but worried about the insurance.

I called for an ambulance, and David said I had no business prancing my *prissy ass* in there with my *high fluting* ideas and he hoped I was prepared to pay for the ambulance and hospital since I made the decision to call without asking him first. I wanted to thank him for making me realize that being an only child wasn't such a bad thing after all, but Clarice had enough to worry about without me picking a fight with her brother.

"Don't listen to him, Rena. The McDaniels' don't accept charity," Clarice looked from Michael to David. "Paying Mama's hospital bill would be charity so you don't need to worry about anything David said." Her voice cracked and I feared the rest of her would follow if she continued to talk with her brother.

"Why don't you check out the contact situation while we wait for the ambulance," I suggested. "It could be a long wait in the emergency room, so you might want to take them out before we go."

She agreed and said I could wait in her bedroom if I didn't want to be near David while she was in the bathroom removing her lenses.

"I'm fine, Clarice. I'm going to call Ann and tell her we won't be back this afternoon."

When I hung up without answering Ann's request for an explanation of why it took both of us to handle Clarice's personal problems, Michael offered me a glass of tea and said he appreciated my help, drawing a sneer from his brother. "If you're planning to drive Clarice to the hospital, would it be okay if I ride along, too?" he asked.

David went into the bedroom off the corner of the living room and did his best to slam the hollow door that didn't have enough power to create a noise.

"Don't pay David no mind," Michael said. "He never learned to control his anger."

Clarice came back in time to open the door for the ambulance personnel.

Chapter 20

Rena stirred up a whole mess of confusion in me. For the time being I was grateful to her for getting sucked into my crazy life without running out when she saw what she got herself into, or hating me for allowing her to come into it. To be perfectly honest, I wasn't sure I could have made it home without her. And she saved me the fuss I would have had with David over calling the ambulance by taking that decision in her own hands.

But I knew, as sure as anything, I was going to wrestle with shame once things settled back to ordinary. I'd worry that she thought I should control how rude David was, or how sick Mama was. Maybe she'd figure I was too much trouble to mess with, or she'd be afraid I was going to wind up as mean as David or as crazy as Mama. I sure couldn't blame her if those thoughts came to her mind after all she had seen on her first visit to the McDaniels home. The keg party I made up would have been better than any little piece of my reality.

At least Michael acted half way respectable. He inherited Daddy's long legs so I told him to sit up front with Rena, knowing he'd never be comfortable in the back seat of her little car. He held the seatback forward while I crawled in and waited for me to settle in before he flipped the seat in my face and sat himself down. I took to noticing every nice thing he did like that, to make up for the hurt David laid on me. The meaner David acted, the nicer I looked at Michael.

Nobody said much on the way to the hospital. I wasn't ready to let Michael horn in on my friendship with Rena on account of I didn't think he earned the right just by being my brother. He still needed to make himself worthy in her eyes by acting like a man. The chance was waiting for him at the hospital if he wanted to take it.

Rena concentrated on driving, but she was polite enough to tell Michael he could adjust the seat or hunt for another station on the radio if he took a notion. I kept still, worrying about Mama, and about missing work, and about paying for the ambulance and hospital bills, and about Rena thinking I was some sort of nut case waiting to develop. A few times, I worried that my tears stained the contacts and messed up Charlotte's gesture with the special.

The ambulance beat us to the hospital, naturally because of having permission to use the siren and lights and speed on through traffic signals and stop signs that caught us. I suspected the girl driver went a little faster than usual even, because Mama's hollering had her jumpy before they got her strapped to the stretcher back at the trailer. She would have been hard pressed to live with it for years on end the way I had.

By the time we got there, they had Mama off somewhere in a real examination room with a door, to keep her from driving the other patients crazy. Rena dropped me and Michael off at the Emergency Room door and went to park her car. The lady at the door said one of us needed to sit down at the counter to register Mama. I figured on that being me, but Michael volunteered. I waited by the door for Rena.

We sat side by side in the back of the waiting room while Michael filled out forms and then he came and sat in a chair across from us. He slumped down in the chair and chewed on his fingernails. Mama tried hard to break him of that habit but never got far with him. I resisted the urge to fuss at him over it since he was worried.

"They want us to try and find Dad," he said. "I told them we tried everywhere we could think of already, and it wouldn't help them much if he showed up anyway since he doesn't have a job or insurance. Or any concern for her."

I tried to signal him with my eyes not to say too much and make Rena feel uncomfortable, figuring it wasn't much fun for her to listen to some other family member spill out all the messy business she had kept secret for so long.

Rena excused herself to go speak to one of the ladies behind the desk. Shortly after, the operator announced for Dr. Boiles to come to the emergency room waiting area.

"That's Rena's dad they just called for," I told Michael. "Maybe we should ask them to call for ours and see which one shows up first."

Michael smiled at me and spit a nail fragment into the air. "Fat chance they'd find him."

Dr. Boiles arrived soon, wearing a white coat. He hugged Rena, said it was nice to see me again, shook Michael's hand – without knowing it had been in his mouth half the morning – and sat down like he had all the time in the world to worry with us. "I'm very sorry to hear about your mother's accident," he said. I wondered if he heard about her dementia too, and was just too polite to mention that part. "She's in good hands with the emergency room physicians, but I'll go back and check on her if it will ease your mind."

I said I'd be grateful, and Michael said yes sir, he would be too. I wanted to say it would be a bigger blessing if he could ease Mama's mind, but he would see that soon enough on his own without me saying a word.

Rena made out like a regular mother hen, trying to take care of us. She walked down to the cafeteria and brought sandwiches and drinks for all of us. She offered to make phone calls if there was anyone we needed to contact, but we couldn't think of one single person who would care to know that our demented mother fell out of bed and rode to St. Mark's Community Hospital in an ambulance.

I finally asked her to call Emily before she left the bank. It would have suited me better to call her myself but I was afraid the nurse might come out to say we could see Mama while I was on the phone. I wrote the bank phone number on a gum wrapper that someone had left on the table beside my chair, and warned Rena about the bank not liking for Emily to get personal calls, so she wouldn't keep her on the phone for long.

I made the right decision because while she was gone outside, away from the noisy waiting room to make her calls, Dr. Boiles came out to get us. "They're pretty sure she fractured her hip." He sounded professional but still like he cared. "You can come back to see her for a minute while she waits for someone from Imaging to come get her for the x-rays."

"Does that hurt her?" What a dummy Dr. Boiles must have thought I was. Of course I knew a fractured hip was bound to hurt her. Why did I ask that question?

"She was given something for pain, and something else for her nerves. She appears to be resting comfortably," he said.

I shot out of my chair, anxious to see her resting comfortably instead of fidgeting and shouting demented nonsense. Michael lagged behind for a spell and I got the idea he wasn't anxious to see her at all. But he followed me and Dr. Boiles through the sliding doors that said no visitors beyond this point.

Rena was in the waiting room when we came back. I told her the news, and that Mama was on her way to have her x-rays taken, and that she was quiet.

"Since everything is under control here," Rena said, "I'm going to leave for a little while and pick Emily up. She wants to be here with you, Clarice."

I big old lump swelled up in my throat, but I managed to talk over it. "I must be the luckiest girl on earth to have two friends like you and Emily." I looked away no more than the words slipped out. Rena surely thought I was a loser for assuming that just because she helped me out, that meant she wanted to jump right into best friend status with Emily.

She leaned over to hug me, and said, "Stay strong while I'm gone."

Michael watched Rena leave through the exit door and stopped gnawing at his fingers long enough to say I must be doing something right to make a friend like Rena. "She don't even care where you came from," he said.

That was the truth. "No, Michael, she doesn't. Rena cares where people are going, not where they came from."

Chapter 21

I remained calm until I had passed through the second set of exit doors and rounded the corner of the building. When shielded from view to the waiting room visitors, I lost everything that resembled composure. My hands shook. My eyes watered, and I bent over at the waist to inhale deadly volumes of exhaust fumes left behind by a busy afternoon of ambulance traffic.

A nurse who had come outside to smoke a cigarette asked if I needed help. I shook my head; afraid if I opened my mouth to speak I might vomit the bile of Clarice's life out of my body.

On second thought, that seemed a better option than trying to find somewhere within to accept it. I stuck my head in the trash container by the door, which I was sure was meant for any purpose other than the one I was using it for, and let go. And go. And go.

The nurse crushed her cigarette under her foot and said to stay right there and she would be right back.

"I'm fine, really," I told her. "I apologize for ruining your break. I'm upset, not sick, really, and I actually feel much better now that I got that out."

"Let me at least get you a wet towel and drink of water," she insisted. "I'll be right back."

My breathing returned to normal while she was inside. I was glad I had waited when she came back; the water tasted good.

"Is it someone you're close to? A family member?" she asked. "I'm used to seeing this reaction after ten years in the emergency room."

"No," I answered, then changed it. "Yes, sort of. I don't know the patient. I met her today. But her daughter is a close friend. I'm upset for her. I guess we know now that I made a wise choice when I decided I didn't want to pursue any career that came close to the medical field. Not only can I not stand the sight of blood, I don't do so well with emotions either. Thanks for your help."

"No problem," she replied. "Are you here with Mrs. McDaniels' daughter?"

"Yes, Clarice McDaniels."

"She seems like a sweet girl. Her poor mother is in pitiful shape. No wonder you're so upset."

I felt defensive. I wanted to tell her that it wasn't Clarice's fault her mother was in pitiful shape. Clarice did the best she could to take care of her mother. I knew that without a doubt, but decided it wasn't necessary to convince the nurse. I thanked her again and left to go get Emily.

~~~

We moved from the emergency waiting room to the surgery area after the doctor confirmed the fractured hip and determined that Michael could legally sign the surgery consent forms since the patient was incompetent and the husband was missing. Michael called home to update David and got no answer. Clarice said she'd bet her last dollar, which I hated to inform her the hospital would claim, that he was at some bar getting smashed *just like his old man would do*. Emily looked at me with sad eyes.

We stayed until nine o'clock, when Mrs. McDaniels was moved from recovery to a private room on the sixth floor. Clarice and Michael went in to visit with her while Emily and I waited in the hall.

"At least she's quiet," Emily said. "That woman screams constantly. It has to be a relief for Clarice to get a night of peace even if she is sorry her mother got hurt. I just hope David doesn't keep her up all night bitching about everything. If I hate anyone, it's him."

"You think he would do that?" I said it like a question, but was fairly certain I already knew the answer.

"Yeah. Clarice doesn't say much. She tries to be all cheerful and pretend everything's okay, but I've known her since first grade and nothing's ever been okay at the McDaniels' house as far as I know. I don't ask questions. I try to let her forget all that and pretend she has a normal life when she gets out of there. I just found out about her mother's dementia."

"I had no idea before today," I admitted. "I feel terrible that she lives through this without talking about it. Do you think she really doesn't want to talk about it, or is she afraid we'll think less of her if she does? How can she keep all that inside?"

"It's hard to say." Emily gave me the impression that she would understand and support Clarice as much as I believed I would.

Mrs. McDaniels' nurse walked out of her room with David and Clarice, telling them to go home and get some rest. "She'll sleep tonight. Everything looks stable and she's comfortable, so there's no reason for you to sit here all night. It's going to be a tough road to recovery and you'll need your energy to help her later."

Clarice blew her nose in a tissue that had begun to disintegrate from being used more times than was intended. I dug through my purse looking for a replacement.

"I'll get something from the nurse's desk," she said. "You stop hunting and run along home. You've done more than enough already. You too, Em. You go home. I'm fine here."

Clarice finished her sentence and then slid down the wall. She buried her head in folded arms over her drawn-up knees and cried. "Good Lord, will the embarrassment ever stop?"

Michael chewed his nails and walked toward the elevator. Emily and I pulled Clarice up, one on each side, and walked her to a seat in the waiting room.

"There's nothing for you to be embarrassed about," I told her. "Emily and I are your friends. We love you." I looked at Emily for reassurance. She nodded confirmation.

"Rena, none of us have a way home," Clarice cried. "We can't expect you to run all over town now to take us home after all you've done already. It's late."

"How about this?" I asked. "Are you ready to drive now?"

She said she was.

"I'll take you back to GWS to get your car, then you can drive Michael and Emily home. That way, you'll have transportation if you need it and you won't have to think I've done too much." I wanted to make sure she could escape if David gave her trouble, as Emily suggested he might.

She agreed to the plan, but Emily came up with another before we got to my car. She wanted Clarice to take Michael home first, and then she could run inside to pick up some things while she was there and go home to spend the night at Emily's house.

Clarice gracefully declined the offer, stating her need to be near the phone as an excuse not to go. "The hospital might call about Mama during the night."

"I'll be there," Michael reminded her.

"Without a car," she shot back. "You won't be able to go if they need you."

What is it with these people? I wondered. Michael doesn't have a car. Emily doesn't have a phone. Mrs. McDaniels doesn't have a mind, and her oldest son and her husband didn't have hearts. Were there people like this everywhere that I had never noticed before?

Emily decided this situation qualified as an emergency. If the hospital called Michael during the night, he could call her downstairs neighbor, who would bang on her ceiling with the broom handle to alert Clarice and Emily that they had a phone call.

It was all settled. I dropped them off at the GWS employee parking lot and told Clarice I would cover the customer service windows alone the next day. She could sit at the hospital with her mother. I watched them get into Clarice's car and waited for her to start the engine and turn the lights on before I left.

And I thought her parents had sheltered her from the ugliness in the world. How wrong I had been. She had seen it all.

Then it hit me, two miles north of GWS, like a ton of bricks. I had the protective parents. At twenty-four I got my first lesson in the real world, and it made me puke. Suddenly protection didn't seem like such a wonderful gift.

I went to my apartment – the place I had never bothered to cozy up until I planned the makeover – because it never felt like a home to me. It was my downscaled replica of the Boiles' museum, devoid of honest emotion. At least Clarice grew up with real live intensity, and her life intertwined with those of the people around her, good or bad. She was part of something. I was sheltered. Opposites again.

I took two Tylenols, scoured my pores and soaked in the tub so I could relax and get to sleep. I had a busy day ahead of me, covering Clarice's window.

~~~

Mother called while I was dressing for work. "Your dad told me what happened with Clarice's mother. Is she okay?"

Unsure which *she* Mother meant, I gave her a brief rundown on each. "Mrs. McDaniels' hip was broken and required surgery. She made it through successfully and was resting comfortably in a private room when we left the hospital shortly after nine." The private room part should have alleviated at least one of Mother's biggest concerns. I remembered when she had a hospital administrator on the phone in the middle of the night once because she couldn't bear the thought of her mother sleeping in a room beside *God knows who* for even one night.

"Clarice was quite shaken up by the accident and exhausted after a long, stressful day. She went home with Emily to spend the night, where I'm sure she was pampered, so she should be rested this morning unless something happened during the night that I don't know about."

"Did you remember to send flowers, Rena? You should send an arrangement on your own, and then take up a collection at the gas company for another. Try to make one fresh cut flowers for fragrance while she's in the hospital, and the other a plant that she can take home to keep."

Should I break the news that Clarice's mother wasn't *in her right mind* and therefore would never know whether or not I sent flowers, so, consequently, I thought it would be more useful to make a donation toward her medical expenses? How would Charlotte Boiles deal with that information? Could she live with the knowledge that her only daughter wanted to break the flower tradition and leave herself, and possibly her mother as well, open to criticism from the garden club? Or would knowing about Clarice's mother's mental status cause her to see Clarice as my *poor little friend* again? I couldn't risk that.

"We didn't leave the hospital until after nine, Mother, and then I had to drive Clarice to GWS to get her car. I really didn't have time to think about flowers," I explained.

"If you will give me the full name and room number, I'll order flowers right away. I'll stop by to visit later, too. I have a light schedule today, so getting away won't be a problem."

Now what? How could I protect Clarice's secret?

"The nurses said the next few days will be rough for Mrs. McDaniels and she won't be ready for a lot of visitors. Last night it was family only, so Emily and I waited in the hall. But I'm sure Clarice would love to see you, and she'll need a break. Maybe you can talk her into leaving the hospital to have lunch with you. I think that would do much more to lift Clarice's spirits. Mrs. McDaniels doesn't know you so she won't expect a visit."

"What an excellent suggestion, Dear. Would you like to join us for lunch?"

Dad must have told her my feelings were hurt when I thought she and Clarice went shopping without inviting me to join them. "I appreciate the invitation, but I think I'll stay in and work through lunch. I'll need the extra time to cover the workload without Clarice."

Mother reminded me that I was legally entitled to a lunch period, regardless of the workload. I said I would keep that in mind. I gave her Mrs. McDaniels' name and room number so she could call Clarice and she said good-bye. But I couldn't let her go.

"Mother, hold on. When did you start wearing glasses?"

She sighed. "You didn't tell her, did you?"

"I didn't give you away," I said. "I came close, though, without meaning to because I wasn't thinking. But I caught on in time."

"Good. After she mentioned that she wanted contacts at the makeover, I wanted to help her get them. I remembered those annoying two-for-one ads that One Step runs frequently and saw the opportunity to help get Clarice out of those hideous rhinestone frames without offering her money."

"It was a good idea," I admitted.

"The problem was, the sale ended before I called. I was so afraid Clarice would know. She remarked a couple of times while we were in there that she was surprised to see so few people had come to take advantage of the offer. I planned to plead ignorance if she asked an employee, or discovered the truth somehow. But she was too excited to give it much thought. I told you, I won't insult her, Rena. And I won't."

"What you did was very nice," I said. "Thank you."

As the day went on, that thank you made me more and more uncomfortable. In saying that, *I* reduced Clarice to *poor little friend* status. How pretentious for me to thank Mother for her kindness to Clarice, as though I owned Clarice, or anything Mother did to help her, somehow helped me.

Ann Lyons came by to tell me that she was taking care of the flower collection for Clarice's mother and to ask how things were going. She offered to call in a temp if Clarice needed an extended leave.

"I'm not sure Clarice's financial situation will allow her much of a leave," I offered, hoping I wasn't betraying her again. "Clarice keeps the details of her life extremely private, but I want to share this piece of information. Yesterday, I learned that she has been supporting her mother, for quite some time."

Ann shook her head. "I honestly had no idea. That might explain the girl's reluctance to spend money on herself, for things like clothes and glasses."

"I'm wondering how the promotion process works at GWS. Clarice has been here for years, and she's a very dedicated, hard worker. How long will she have to work here before she starts to climb the ladder?" I asked. "I would like to see her follow in the footsteps of our industrious CEO."

"Rena, all open positions are posted daily on the bulletin board outside my office for review. Clarice is welcome, as are all employees, to apply for any position she desires. She has yet to do so, even though I have encouraged her to every year during her evaluation. For some reason, she seems content to stay where she is."

I said I would try to encourage Clarice when she returned to work. Meanwhile, I would relay the information about extended leave when I saw her later at the hospital.

Several customers asked about Clarice and sent well wishes when I told them that her mother was in the hospital recovering from an emergency surgery. I wrote their names on my calendar so I would remember to tell her they cared.

I worked thirty minutes over to make sure the paperwork was caught up and things were ready for the next day, and then went directly to the hospital. I had planned to take Clarice to the cafeteria and buy her dinner, but she had already eaten.

"The nurse brought me a tray," she said. "Seeing how Mama isn't allowed any food yet and she's entitled to a meal with her room charge. Girlfriend, the food is good enough to make people want to be sick just so they can stay here and eat. I had prime rib, baked potato, asparagus, a Caesar salad, and chocolate crème pie for dessert."

"You're right," I said. "I almost want to break a bone to get that." I was sure one of my parents probably had something to do with the meal, but didn't say so to Clarice.

"Poor Michael's in the cafeteria eating his heart out," she said. "If you want to join him, I'll go with you."

In the elevator, she told me that her mother had slept quietly for most of the day. "They're keeping her knocked out so she won't get restless and hurt herself again, but in a few days they have to let her wake up so they can try to get her out of bed. I don't think I want to be in earshot when that time comes. The doctor says she'll be here for at least five days."

"Before I forget, things are fine at work. Ann understands if you need to be here and said to call her to discuss an extended leave if that becomes necessary."

"Okay, I'll think about it," she said, and changed the subject as quickly as I had. "Did you know your Mama was here earlier? She said I needed a break, which I did because it's boring as all get out watching Mama sleep and Michael chew his nails, so she took me to lunch at Pizza Hut. That's my favorite restaurant."

I didn't tell her Mother hates pizza.

I paid for my vegetable lasagna and large coke and we joined Michael at his table by the far wall. His napkin lay crumpled on top of a half-eaten hamburger while he chewed on his hands.

"I tried to call David again," Clarice told him. "Still no answer." To me she said, "David didn't come home all night." I appreciated that they included me in the family discussion, like I belonged.

"Maybe he's run out like the old man," Michael said. "He probably saw the writing on the wall and figured there'd be more work and lots of bills when she gets out of here. That's two things David ain't going to stick around to face up to."

"Fine with me," Clarice said.

"Clarice, you need to get your head back on straight," Michael warned. "The barges come back in next week and then I'm out of here for three or four weeks. You can't take care of Mama alone."

"My head's just fine, Michael. But I can only fret over one problem at a time. Today, it's getting Mama well."

I remembered Jansen's one-problem-a-day limit, and smiled. "Way to go Clarice. Keep it simple. Another suggestion, if you're accepting them, is to take some time for yourself, too."

"I'll accept your suggestion," she said.

"While your mother's in here where she is being taken care of by nurses, how about we call Jansen for our first dance lesson? I hear dancing is great for stress relief."

Michael looked at me like I was crazy. "You can come too, I told him. "If you reduce your stress level, you might stop eating your fingers."

He shook his head. "I guess you're gonna take Mama's place with the nagging, huh?"

He looked to Clarice to catch her reaction, and she said it sounded good to her, as long as it wasn't on Emily's class night. And Michael could come if he wanted.

I called Jansen when I got home and told him about Clarice's mother's surgery, and that we wanted to set up a dance lesson as soon as he was available. He suggested we do it on Friday night, and that way we could go out somewhere to dance afterwards.

Chapter 22

Clarice returned to work on Thursday, insisting that she needed the money, and even more needed the peace of mind.

"Mama's awake and hollering out worse than ever. She drove the nurses plum out of their minds. And other patients fussed about the noise and asked for transfers to different floors. Mama takes some getting used to before you can sleep through her racket. She caused the nurses a lot of extra work, in addition to wearing out their nerves, so I don't blame them for getting upset with her."

"Did they discontinue her sedatives?" I asked.

"They still give her some, but not as much. Now they keep her tied to the bed because she swats at the nurses and tries to get up. I'm embarrassed, Rena. I'm ashamed to walk out the door of her room and have people stare at me like I'm the daughter of the wacko, which I am, and I'm embarrassed for her to mistreat the people who are trying to take care of her. I'm wasting my time up there because she doesn't even know I'm around. So I'm better off coming back to work."

"Welcome back," I said. "I missed you. And, believe me, I noticed the difference when you weren't here. You do way more than half of the work."

I updated her on the status of the filing and showed her where I left off on her list of delinquent calls. "And before I forget," I ripped a page out of my calendar and handed it to her, "these people all left well wishes for you and a speedy recovery for your mother."

She looked at me with fear on her face, and I assured her that I hadn't mentioned the dementia, only that her mother had an emergency hip replacement.

"Is your mother in pain?" I asked.

"Who knows?" Clarice sounded discouraged. "The doctor called in a whole slew of specialists, some of them to check out her dementia and see if they can figure out how to control her agitation."

She paused long enough to shuffle the papers on her desk and rearrange her supplies, all of which ended up in their original position, the way she always did when she had something to say but either couldn't decide how to say it or didn't want to say it.

"What's wrong, Clarice? I know all that shuffling means you have something on your mind. You can tell me anything, you know."

"A social worker came in to talk to me and Michael yesterday. Talk about humiliating. I hate Daddy more than ever for leaving us open to an investigation by social services, like we're orphans or abusive children to our diapered mother. I wanted to crawl under a rock and hide when she came in."

I tried to imagine hospital rooms equipped with giant rocks to crawl under when things became too uncomfortable to bear, and decided hospitals would need to be built in caves if that were something they offered. Their whole purpose is to house people who are uncomfortable.

"The hospital employs social workers," I told her. "They aren't state workers who are only called when something is amiss. They're also used to help solve problems that are beyond anyone's control, or to assist families with long-term planning."

"You don't think the state sent her to investigate why we let Mama fall?"

"No, Clarice, you have a tremendous amount of responsibility on your shoulders. I'm sure they want to help. And I think you should let them."

She blinked rapidly, to clear away the moisture from her eyes, unlike the slow blink she used to realign her contact lenses

"Charity is going to pay the hospital bill." She blinked some more and fanned her hands in front of her eyes. "I don't want to cry on these contacts again and get everything looking blurry here at work."

She took a deep breath, wiped her mouth, and spoke with determined control. "Mama would rather be dead than accept charity, but I don't know how else I can ever pay for the surgery. Michael said he thought on the subject all night, and he thinks maybe it was just Daddy who was dead set against charity, and Mama only went along to keep the peace. He could be onto something, because Mama never did have much of a mind of her own."

I thought that might explain why she had given it up so easily, but it felt unfair considering I had only met her a few days before.

"For years," Clarice continued, "I figured Mama had a streak of imagination hidden somewhere on account of she made up the name *Clarice*. I felt proud because she took the time to think up a special name for me after she gave David and Michael ordinary names. Come to find out, my name was just another example of her refusing to put her foot down for what she wanted. She wanted to name me Clara, for her mother. But Daddy pitched one of his fits and said he wanted to name me for his mother, Bernice. Mama mixed up the two names, giving Clara the front seat, of course, but not sticking up for Clara.

"I like your name." I pointed out that it was original by telling her I had never met anyone else with her name.

"I liked it better before I came into the truth about it." She shook her head like she couldn't believe her mother had betrayed her own mother this way. "Anyhow, Michael might be right about charity being something else Mama didn't really agree with Daddy on, but she didn't want to fight him on it since we didn't have any need to collect charity at the time."

I didn't know Mrs. McDaniels when she had any mind of her own, so I couldn't honestly know what to think about her position on accepting charity. But I thought I knew that Clarice needed to believe Michael on this issue or she might destroy herself with guilt.

"It sounds like Michael has thought this through," I said. "If your mother had a history of doing whatever it took to keep peace, and your father objected to accepting assistance, it's very likely that she didn't share his opinion. She probably chose not to voice her opposition because she wanted to save her energy for a more important battle. I think I'm with Michael on this one."

She stared at nothing and bobbed her head slightly.

"Your mother wouldn't ask you to suffer unnecessarily on her behalf, would she?"

"No." Clarice answered without a moment of hesitation. "She suffered a lot of the time to protect us. She still would, if she could."

"Then I'm sure she wouldn't want you to spend the rest of your life trying to pay off her medical expenses. I think she would accept the charity for herself to make things easier for you."

Clarice rubbed her temples and asked me if my mother would want me to accept charity on her behalf.

My brain scrambled. At first I couldn't envision a situation in which I might be offered charity, on my mother's behalf or my own. "I'm thinking," I told her; so she wouldn't think I was ignoring her.

I remembered a time when the neighbors got together in someone's garage at the end of every summer to exchange children's clothing. The kids stood aside and observed while the parents swapped outgrown school uniforms and barely used dress clothes. We didn't participate. Mother boxed my things up and took them to a homeless shelter. She claimed our neighbors could afford new clothes for their children and the parents of those poor little shelter children needed my hand-me-downs. Iris Bell said Mother did that because she thought I was too good to wear anything that had been worn by someone else first, and that was Mother's way of getting out of the exchange party without looking like a snob.

Using that as a reference, I decided Mother would hold the same opinion as Mr. McDaniels. I didn't want to admit that to Clarice, so I searched for another example that might change my mind, finally coming up with something.

"I know my mother would be very sad if I were in a position to need assistance, and the one thing that could actually put my family in that position would be a medical emergency. There are circumstances that go beyond insurance company limits, and procedures that are still considered experimental so insurance doesn't cover them at all."

"But your family would never run out of money." Clarice stated that as though it were an indisputable fact and she dared me to refute it and disillusion her.

"I don't know," I mused. "There are several things that could wipe out any family. A transplant, or a horrible legal situation comes to mind. For example, Mother knew of a man who a jury found guilty of a murder he didn't commit. He lost everything, and his wife ended up selling their home and using the money from the house, plus all of their savings, to pay his legal fees. When the truth came out, the state gave him a miniscule fraction of what he lost. His wife and kids received food stamps and medical assistance during part of his incarceration."

"That's horrible," Clarice said. "I guess I never gave much thought to people being able to lose everything when they live in a house like the one you grew up in."

"When I think about these possibilities, I know my Mother would rather I accept assistance on her behalf than watch me suffer without something I need in order to pay her medical or legal fees." As the words came from my mouth, I was surprised to realize I actually believed them. "Mothers never want to cause their children pain."

Clarice brightened her expression without giving in to a real smile. "So you think Mama wants me to accept the charity for her now instead of going into debt to pay the medical bills?"

"That's exactly what I think." I said. "And I guess that's what Michael believes as well. Clarice, I have a good idea what your salary is, and you would be paying for the rest of your life without making a dent in the total."

She dropped her head. "There's more. The doctor told me to prepare myself because he doesn't think Mama will be able to go home when she leaves the hospital. He said she'll be harder to take care of, and he doesn't think I can handle her."

I could see that the thought of this was tearing her apart. "I'm so sorry, Clarice," was all I could think of to say since I tended to believe that her mother was more than she should have been expected to handle before.

"If she cooperates, which we both know she won't," Clarice said, "she could go to a rehab center for a while to learn how to get out of bed and into a wheel chair, or maybe even walk to the bathroom again. If not, he wants to send her to a nursing home."

She blinked and fanned her eyes some more. "I can't talk about it now."

"Okay," I said. "Let's return to your normally scheduled program. Are you driving in your contacts now?"

She was driving in them and had worked up to a full day with no problem. "I pop them in and out as easy as a piece of cake," she said, beaming through the tears still on her face.

"When are we going to cut the layers in my hair?" I asked, surprised by how much I had to trust her to even consider allowing her to do this.

"Name your time, Girlfriend, and I'll be there. I'll do it today during lunch if you want."

"I'm not skipping another lunch," I told her. "How about Friday night? We can make a full night of it. You guys can come to my apartment after work and I'll order pizza. Then you can cut my hair before Jansen comes for our dance lesson. And then we can go out to show off our new looks – your contacts, my hair cut, and our dancing."

"We'll knock 'em dead." She smiled. "It would be really cool if our makeup comes in before then.

As an afterthought she double-checked to make sure Michael was still invited to join us. "He's been extra nice lately," she said, and I could tell that made her happy.

~~~

I called Jen to confirm that the dance lesson was still on, and told her everything that was going on with Clarice's mother. She called Angela, who miraculously amassed my entire party order and delivered it to Jen to bring to the pizza party on Friday.

Clarice seemed to relax when she walked into the apartment and saw that the mess from last week's party was still stacked on the dining room table. "Look, Michael, she's trying to impress you with her good housekeeping skills. She keeps house just like you do."

I laughed. "I cleaned before the party. Don't tell me you expected me to clean afterwards, too. There's only so much a girl can change at a time."

Clarice's mood lightened more after I teased back, but mine went the opposite direction. I realized I had changed considerably in the few weeks since I had started planning that makeover party. In all the confusion over Mother wanting to change Clarice, and my fight to defend her right to remain as she was, I was the one who had changed the most. But I didn't have time to dissect it; my guests waited and the pizza was on the way.

I grabbed the tablecloth that Angela has used on the folding table the week before, shook it out, and spread it in the living room floor. "We'll have a picnic," I called over my shoulder as I went to the kitchen for paper plates and napkins.

Clarice and Michael had already moved to the floor when I came back. Emily was in the dining room picking up the candles. "May as well make it a fancy picnic," she said, placing the candles in the center of the tablecloth.

Clarice giggled, almost returning to the innocent state she was in the first day she came in to work wearing her contact lenses. "I never heard of a picnic in the house before, but I'll play along."

"Probably because we didn't have room," Michael said.

The doorbell rang and Jen yelled from the hall. "Hurry up, my hands are full."

Michael, who was closest to the door, opened it and took the pizza boxes from her hands before she dropped the bags of cosmetics stuffed under her arms. "I ran into the delivery boy in the parking lot and thought I'd be Ms. Nice," she said. "I nearly dropped everything trying to open the outside door. Who are you? I'm Jen, Rena's friend."

"I'm Michael, Clarice's brother."

"And Rena's friend too," I corrected. "Or did you only agree to come along with us because Clarice forced you?"

"No," he said, self-consciously. "I'm Rena's friend also."

"We're having a picnic," Clarice told Jen.

"I see. Looks like Rena's table is too stacked up to eat from again. I hope those mirrors are still over there because I brought the makeup."

Clarice squealed, and I wasn't sure she was going to be able to sit still long enough to eat before she dug into the bags. Emily and I went to fix drinks while Jen calmed Clarice and doled out the plates and napkins. Michael pulled a lighter from his pocket and lit the candles.

Michael watched Clarice carefully while we ate, as though, instead of living with her since the day she was born, he had never seen her before. Finally, he asked her if she could imagine how, if they had had room, their father would have reacted if their mother had spread a blanket on the floor and had a picnic in the house.

They both laughed until Clarice had tears rolling down her face and Michael was holding his stomach. Emily and Jen laughed, probably more at the way they were laughing than the subject. I wanted to cry, because I thought that's what their laughter truly represented; a situation too sad to cry about so they released the hurt in the only other way they knew how.

"You two make me wish I had a brother again," I said.

"You used to have a brother?" Clarice sounded shocked. Jen looked at me like I was crazy.

"No, but I wanted one all of my life, until I met David. He killed that dream for me, but Michael is bringing it back to life."

His eyes covered over briefly, and he blinked to clear them. "Thank you, Rena. That means a lot to me."

Clarice stopped laughing but remained cheerful. "Glory be, Rena, you brought out some emotion in Michael. That's got to be a miracle."

"I think it's probably because I'm the only male in the room," Michael said. "All your mushy stuff is wearing off on me. If the truth be known, Rena, I ain't been the greatest brother in the world to Clarice. Me and David both gave her a hard way to go." He looked at her like he wished he could change that.

"That's what made me strong," Clarice told him. "I wouldn't have it any other way. But from here on out you can be nice. I'm strong enough now."

Jen went to the bathroom. I think she was getting emotional, and that might have been a second miracle.

I told everyone to grab another slice of pizza if they wanted more so I could clean up the picnic and turn the room into a dance floor. Clarice cleared the table and pulled the makeup mirrors out of their boxes.

"I want to put my makeup on before we have the dance lesson if it's okay. That way I'll feel like someone else," she said, looking at Michael. "Hopefully somebody with rhythm."

I said sure and that it wouldn't hurt my feelings if she wanted to wait until another time to cut my hair so we could spend more time with makeup. She was relieved. With her contacts in, and under Michael's direction instead of Mother's, she applied her makeup, again to cover-girl perfection. Michael said he was glad he was going to be around to chaperone.

By the time Jansen showed up, we were sufficiently beautiful and giddy to make his job enjoyable. He said he couldn't believe it was the first time Michael had danced swing, and that he must be a natural. Clarice was proud, and Michael embarrassed.

"I can just hear what the guys at Grayson's would say if they could see you now," Clarice teased.

"Or the old man," Michael said. "No offense, Jansen, but he would disown me." They broke into another round of cleansing laughter.

"The guys at Grayson's won't ever see this unless I end up on the big screen TV," he said, and they laughed harder. "They never get more than a mile outside of Shady Acres."

Clarice stopped laughing and shot him a look of horror, which I read to say no more mention of Shady Acres. But it was too late. Michael's comment hadn't gone unnoticed.

"Shady Acres?" Jansen asked. "On Highway 24?"

"Yeah," Michael answered, and sent an apologetic look his sister's way.

"Grayson's Pub? Home of the famous big screen and infamous heartburn barbecue sandwiches? Grayson is my uncle. I lived in Shady Acres until I was five years old."

"No shit?" Michael looked at Jansen as though trying to remember him but coming up blank. "We had to be there at the same time. I know you are younger than me. Do you remember him Clarice?"

She shook her head.

"I'm twenty-five, Jansen said. "You probably never saw me. I wasn't allowed to play outside. We were at the end of Elm, by the playground. I used to watch out the window and wish I could play with everyone else but my mother was over-protective. I had asthma and I wore some sort of contraption on my legs. They turned in when I was born and we didn't have insurance to fix them until I was three."

"Well, you've sure overcome the problem," Jen said. "The way you dance I'd never guess."

"I've overcome many problems since then," Jansen said. "But I won't bore you with all the details. Let's dance."

We practiced in my living room until Jansen swore we would put all the other dancers at Dancing in the Street to shame. Michael learned how to flip Emily over his arm.

I wanted to send them off to have a good time, and go to bed. Instead, I added a fresh coat of my new lipstick to my fake smile and said I was ready.

Chapter 23

Emily rode to Dancing in the Street with Jen so she wouldn't have to walk alone if we had to park clear on the other side of town like we did the last time. Michael rode with me so he could chaperone and make like he was my bodyguard. I didn't mind since he was acting nice, and, if I'm totally honest, I let myself be flattered by him acting like I looked good enough to need protection.

We all tried to talk Rena into riding in our cars so she wouldn't be alone but she was headstrong about driving her own car. She insisted that she felt lucky about getting in the real parking lot. But Jansen followed her in his car just in case her luck ran out.

Michael wore my ears out on the way, talking more in those twenty minutes than he had in the last twenty years, so far as saying anything I wanted to hear anyway. He told me I looked *real* pretty again and said he wasn't only telling me that to be nice, he meant it. He told me he liked my friends, including Jansen who was *a little too girly* for his liking, but decided that might be on account of his Mama being so overprotective. I figured Michael's opinion was on account of his daddy being a little overugly about matters like this.

The real shocker, though, Michael saved until we found a parking space and were fixing to get out of the car. "Rena," he said, "when I start drawing my paychecks from the barge, I'm aiming to help you pay to get the braces on your teeth."

I nearly dropped my teeth right then and there and saved him the expense. I said, "Huh," just so he'd have to repeat it because I wasn't depending on my hearing that straight otherwise.

"I started thinking on it after Jansen said what he did about not getting his legs fixed until they got insurance, and about getting out of Shady Acres and making changes in his life. It ain't fair to you that Daddy never got a job with insurance to fix your teeth, or that he drank up his money instead of dropping it in that orange juice bottle you carted around. You've been wanting out of Shady Acres all along. It started way back when you were a kid and you planned all these years how to do it."

I wanted to hug him. It took a minute to stop my heart from pounding half out of my chest before I could speak. "Michael, that was one of the nicest things anybody ever said to me, including Mama. But I can't take your money. I've been saving up on my own and between that and the insurance I get at GWS, I'll have enough soon to get braces."

I still couldn't get over being raised not to accept charity and I wasn't sure if brothers counted as charity.

"Clarice, you almost made it out on your own. If it wasn't for helping out with Daddy's responsibilities, you would have done it already. You won't be at Shady Acres forever. I can see that now. This ain't charity for you. I want to do the old man's part. It's charity toward him. If you had a Daddy that helped you out like other girls, you'd be prettier than all of them."

I appreciated that coming from Michael, and told him so. But I told him to stop talking like that because I didn't want to get all blubbery and smear my makeup or make my contacts blurry.

He ignored my warning. "Thanks for asking me to come out with you and your friends, Clarice. I'm real sorry about Mama being sick and all, but the one good thing about it is I got to know you a little better."

"That's good, Michael. Mama would want us to find a silver lining."

He kept on talking while we walked over to Dancing in the Street. "Have any of the other girls laid claim to Jansen yet," he asked. "If not, you might ought to take an interest in him yourself."

I just kept walking like I didn't hear that.

"I went along with David when he teased you and said all that Cinderella shit, but I didn't mean most of what I said. You'll make somebody a good wife. You don't need to waste any more of your time taking care of Mama or David or me."

"Do you think Jansen would give me a second thought?" I asked. "I got the idea lots of girls are running after him last time we went dancing. Wait until you see him dancing in there with all kinds of cute girls before you go thinking he'd look at me."

Michael should know my history with boys. It wasn't good. Boy to be accurate, since I only had one boyfriend. I fell in love with Randy Morgan in sixth grade and stayed that way for six whole years. He loved me back clean through ninth grade. Then his daddy found out who my daddy was and said Randy couldn't get hooked up with me, on account of Daddy had sucker-punched one of Mr. Morgan's church buddies in the parking lot at the Dairy Mart. Daddy said the man hit him with the exit door on his way out and walked off without saying excuse me. Randy's version of the story didn't include anything about the exit door, and it was easier to believe the word of the church man. Daddy imagined might near everybody he ever passed had committed some sort of mishap against him, even if it was as meaningless as having a smart-assed look on their face.

"Do you think David is going to follow right along in Daddy's footprints?" I asked, figuring he knew David better than I ever would or would want to. "For a few days after Daddy left, my heart kind of warmed up to David. I thought he might turn around and head straight, but it didn't last long."

Michael kicked a rock off the sidewalk onto the street. "Somebody could turn their ankle," he explained when I looked at him like he was turning into a kid again. "I think David will be back. The nurse said someone came to see Mama the other night after visiting hours were over. It sounded like David but whoever it was didn't want to give up his name. David probably knew Mama wouldn't recognize his name anyway."

"We would have known, though," I said. "He could have left a message for us."

By this time we were almost to the club. Michael stopped, probably not wanting strangers to hear our conversation. "He needs to work this out in his head, Clarice. That's how David operates. He goes off somewhere to think things through. He's got a lot to think on this time. Like how he's going to get by if he doesn't get a job. You laid us straight when you threatened to cut us off, you know."

"I wasn't aiming to chase him off. I wanted him to pull his own weight is all."

Michael told me not to let it keep me awake at night; I did the best thing in his mind. "If Mama would have done that to Daddy a long time ago, or Daddy to us, we'd all be a heap better off for it."

I wanted to be upset with him for talking that way about Mama while she was laid up in the hospital with a broken hip, but I couldn't rightly draw up the anger. I knew he was right.

"Do you think that's why she lost her mind?" I asked. "Because she wasn't strong enough to run her life the way she knew it should be? I think she just hung on until she got me through school. Maybe I should have gone on to college so she would have kept her mind a little longer."

"She made it look that way, Clarice. I know you want to protect her, and it's nice to keep on loving her the way you do. But sooner or later you need to open your eyes up to the truth about her. She let you down as much as he did."

I threw my hand up and said stop. "I'm serious, Michael, don't say any more right now because I'll cry. You can tell me all that another time."

We walked up right behind Emily and Jen in the line to get in Dancing in the Street. The same wrestler looking man checked our ID with his flashlight and I thought he gave Michael a funny look when he handed him the state issued identification card instead of a driver's license. After he walked on back in the line, I told Michael I wanted to teach him to drive. Now that he was going to work on the barge, he'd be able to save up and buy a car.

"You're counting on that barge paying me a lot of money aren't you?" he asked. "It wouldn't hurt for me to get my license anyway, though. Thanks."

I pulled Emily aside and asked her if it was weird to swing dance with my brother. I didn't want to break any rules or appear perverted. She said she didn't see anything wrong with it. She used to dance on her daddy's feet when she was little and nobody made anything of it.

"I just don't want him to stand around and get bored if he's too shy to ask any girls to dance," I told her. She promised she would dance with him. She would even ask him first if he didn't ask her.

Chapter 24

When everyone else left, I stayed behind to load glasses in the dishwasher, and bag paper plates and pizza boxes, wondering how I was going to shake Jansen. I could give in and ride with him but then I'd feel obligated to stay until closing time and I was sure I wouldn't want to do that. Or, I could park blocks away like everyone else and feel like a burden later when he insisted on walking me back to my car because I wanted to leave early.

Neither choice excited me. I ended up telling him I needed to make a stop on the way, and preferred to keep it private. He consented, reluctantly, probably thinking I had a secret lover or drug problem, and drove off without me.

I gave Jansen a ten-minute head start and then drove straight to the Dancing in the Street parking lot where I tipped Kyle Brady three dollars. He waved me into one of the parking spaces he reserved for his old classmates. I stopped and made the required promise of secrecy, and told him I felt like a liar and a bigger jerk each time my friends parked blocks away and then got together to discuss how lucky I am to always get a place in the lot.

"You'll get me in big trouble if anyone finds out," he reminded me.

"I know. And everyone from dear old Southern will hate me for ruining a good thing," I said. "You should appreciate my silence, Kyle. I don't care what any of them think of me, or if I ever come back to this place so my silence is totally out of dedication to you."

He gave me thumbs up and said he loved me.

190

Kyle represented my true luck. Finally, a man professed his love for me, and it had to be someone whose ambition was to buy friends by hustling parking spaces at Dancing in the Street. No wonder I gave up on men.

I hated Dancing in the Street more each time I went there but entered the madhouse determined to make the best of the situation for Clarice's sake. She was anxious to show off her new dance, and her new contacts, and her new makeup. I suspected she was also excited about exploring her new friendship with her brother. I would enjoy watching Clarice have a good time, and for that reason alone I was glad to be there.

That's probably how Mother felt all those hundreds of hours when she sat on bleachers and folding chairs, watching my tennis lessons and dance classes. Ouch. I suffered a stab that closely resembled phantom pain, although I wasn't sure the pain stemmed from anything I had truly lost. I don't think I ever truly owned the assurance that Mother didn't care in the first place.

I hadn't planned to bring Mother to Dancing in the Street with me, but there she was settling in my head again. I was more surprised to find myself admitting to myself that I had more in common with her than with the hordes of young people pushing and screaming around me.

Jen and Emily had arrived first, and proudly secured a table beside the dance floor since we had crossed over from wallflowers to somewhat-experienced swing dancers. I smiled my greeting because it was so loud the person next to me wouldn't have been able to hear me scream if I had tried to get my voice through. And I sat in my prized dance-floor adjacent chair while people bumped against it as they fought their way through the crowd to claim prime space on the floor.

The waitresses didn't pretend they were willing to brave their way through the rowdy mob with a tray of drinks, so we went to the bar to serve ourselves, and hoped to make it back to the table without having our drinks knocked out of our hands. I questioned my sanity when I remembered that I had willingly parted with a cover charge in order to buy the privilege of sitting in a smoke filled room with lights flashing in my face and chaos surrounding me.

I couldn't blame a second of the discomfort I suffered that night on Jansen or Michael, who proved that it's human nature to want what someone else has. Unattached males lined the room and filled the bar, but Jansen and Michael seemed to be the main attractions with the single females, simply because they had come with females who were showering them with attention. They were too busy to notice, carefully dividing their time between their four dates to make sure we all got to dance often, and kept drinks on the table. But I noticed the attention they were getting.

Clarice wore a huge smile. She danced every turn she got, and I gave her a few of mine. Several times, other guys from the sidelines asked her to dance when Jansen and Michael were busy with Jen and Emily. Michael kept a close eye on her when she danced with strangers.

When I felt confident that no one would miss me or think I was rude if I left, and I would die if I had to stay much longer, I said good night and allowed Michael to walk me to my car. He held my hand and led me through the crowd, taking the majority of bumps for me. When we got to the door, he opened it and held it while I passed through.

I wondered about Mrs. McDaniels. From all I had heard, David was a younger, nicer version of Mr. McDaniels. Clarice and Michael were opposites of him, so they must have been like their mother. How could a woman who was like Clarice have stayed with a man who was like David, or like the Mr. McDaniels I imagined? Does the weaker of an opposite pair always lose forfeit sanity if they stay in the relationship too long?

I felt sorry for Mrs. McDaniels, and for Michael and Clarice, that she hadn't been the stronger personality in the relationship so she could influence her husband positively instead of the other way around. Thank goodness Clarice developed so much strength. She would never throw her life away on someone who didn't deserve her.

That thought relieved me. And, then, Mother came back to sit in my thoughts. She must have been stressed the whole time I lived through my Keith Warner, Scott Moran, and Matthew what's-his-name phase, hoping I was strong enough not to end up like them.

Kyle waved as we passed, so I told Michael I would be fine if he wanted to go back inside. "Jansen won't be able to keep up with three girls on his own."

"He'll be fine," Michael assured me. "If you have a minute, I'd like to talk to you." He looked at the ground and added, "About Clarice."

"I'll be heading out soon to work on the barge," he started. "I'll be gone for weeks at a time. I don't want Clarice living in the trailer alone with David while I'm gone."

"Oh, I hadn't thought of that," I told him. "It doesn't sound like very pleasant living conditions."

"I don't think Mama will be back. Even if she is," he said, "she's too much trouble for Clarice to handle alone. Will you talk to her for me?"

"What should I say?" I asked.

"Tell her she needs to break out on her own like you did. Get an apartment. Maybe she can talk Emily into moving out with her or something. Tell her to find a husband. Make a life. Anything," he said. "Help Clarice be strong enough to stand on her own and tell her to forget about keeping up that dump for me and David to live in."

I stood in confused silence while I sorted through what he had said. Me? He was asking *me* to tell *Clarice* to be strong?

"Michael, I don't think you understand. I didn't move out on my own because I was strong. I moved out because I was too weak to work on my relationship with my mother, and escaping was easier. I turn to Clarice for strength, hoping that someday I will understand where she gets hers."

"Will you talk to her?" He sounded almost desperate.

"Sure," I promised. "Maybe we should talk to her together. She respects your opinion as much as mine."

He said thank you and helped me into my car. I watched him walk away, and noticed that he spoke to Kyle as he walked past the little wooden shack where he waited out the night until everyone came back to get their cars. I thought Clarice was lucky to have Michael for a brother, and realized that I, too, was lucky I had been drawn into their family. They accepted me. I could share this brother instead of regretting the fact that I didn't have one of my own.

I looked at the clock on my dash. My parents would have been in bed for hours. Otherwise, I might have dropped by.

Just to visit.

From the Author:

I hope you enjoyed reading Rena's Silver Lining even a fraction as much as I enjoyed writing it. This story came to me in a dream. I woke in the middle of the night filled with dream-hangover concern for the girl in my dream. Hard as I tried, I couldn't figure out who she was. Nor could I go back to sleep.

So, I started writing. Rena and Clarice both became real characters to me before morning. The story poured out and I did little else until this book was written. Still, it was a while before I realized that these characters represented the struggle I was having with the difference between the mother I had always loved and the mother she had turned into as her mind slipped.

I welcome feedback (sandyknauermorgan@gmail.com), and will appreciate ratings and reviews. If you enjoyed this story, please recommend it to family and friends.

Included at the end of this book is a preview of **Song in My Heart**.

Song in My Heart

Sandy Knauer Morgan

Chapter 1

In one of her worst departures from sanity, Momma threw her keys at me and laughed. "Go ahead since you think you're so big. Driving ain't as easy as you think."

I left the keys where a crack in the linoleum had interrupted their skid an inch from my bare foot, refusing to even look at them. Momma couldn't have been serious, and I wasn't falling for another of her tricks. I waited, twisting my fingers, for her next cue. She hooked her thumbs in her armpits and flapped her arms. "Chicken," she mocked, following with cackling sounds. "You're too big a chicken to even try."

She spun around to start her songs over on the hi-fi, goading me with more chicken imitations as she lifted the arm and raised the records. I held my breath. A record dropped, the needle skipped over to connect in a groove, and music blared through the scratchy speaker before I dared believe she might be serious.

Maybe it was the one time that I could be grateful she didn't listen carefully to what I said. She was wrong; I didn't said I thought I was so big, or I wanted to drive the car that very day. What I said was I thought my cousin Wanda was lucky. Uncle Bobby had given her a key to his farm truck and permission to drive through the field between their house and Nana and Pappy's house, in celebration of her turning ten and having legs long enough to reach the pedals.

Momma's nature didn't encourage the notion to be nice or fun very often so I took advantage of the opportunity while I had it. I pulled the keys closer with my foot and kept my eyes on her while I squatted to scoop them up, prepared to innocently hand them over if she turned around.

She forgot about the keys and sang along with Connie Francis. I backed out of the house, carefully holding the screen door until it closed, to keep it from slamming. Pappy called that door the disgrace of Crayfield County, since the screen part had been missing for as long as I could remember. The only purpose the door served was to slam and let everyone know someone had come or gone, sort of like the bell hanging on the door at the bakery. I didn't want to announce my departure to my mother, or my grandmother in the next house.

I waited on the porch--crouched beside the door--for the next record change, to make sure Momma wasn't coming after me. Music claimed most of her attention, playing from the minute Daddy left for work until he came back at suppertime and turned it off, sometimes asking if she aimed to bust my eardrums and sometimes claiming it gave him a headache. Either way, he wasted his breath. I had heard those songs so many times they stayed in my head long after he shut off the power, and she'd find another way to antagonize his headaches.

When I finally decided the coast was clear, I tore out as fast as I could run. My feet hardly touched the ground as I ran to the end of the rutted dirt drive, across the grass to the edge of our property, and up to where Momma parked her old Chevy.

I grabbed the door handle and heard Nana's voice screeching from across the field. "Stop right where you are, Penny Sue Martox!" Nana meant business when she tacked Martox onto the end of my name. I sucked in a quick breath and my heart thumped like a trapped jackrabbit inside my sun suit, but I didn't turn toward her. With my thumb glued to the chrome button on the door handle, I carefully reviewed the situation and its potential consequences.

She was too far off to have seen or heard my reactions, and too fair to hold me responsible for a command that I hadn't heard. However, she might insist that I should have known better than to get in Momma's car, even without her warning, and spit out a few of her favorite threats. I let them echo in my head while I considered what to do next.

"*I ought to tan your hide, Penny Sue.*" No, she wouldn't.

"*I have a notion to box your ears for not listening, little girl.*" No, she wouldn't.

"*I swear, child, I should haul you up to the funny farm and have your fool head examined.*" Never.

I deserved all of them if I proceeded, but knew the worst Nana would actually deliver would be a threat, and maybe a lecture. Consistency was the main thing that set my grandmother apart from my parents, and one of the things I loved the most about her.

Some of her consistencies were good, like her big heart and the way she protected me. Some weren't so good, like her big mouth and the way she protected me. I was much older before I understood how the same thing could be both good and bad, but even back then I was smart enough to appreciate knowing exactly where she stood with everything and everybody, and what to expect from her.

Nana fried chicken on Sunday and breaded pork chops on Wednesday. She scrubbed the porches with bleach water and a brush on Saturday and painted them in May, right after she planted tomatoes. She ironed everything in the house on Tuesday. Her right eyelid fluttered like a hummingbird's wing when she had problems on her mind. If she was wearing anything except pastel pedal pushers, she was going in town or to church. She loved Daddy and me every minute of her life, and didn't like Momma for one second of any day.

I didn't let on but I knew that she watched me like a hawk from behind her ruffled kitchen curtains every time I played outdoors. She worried I would break my neck when I climbed the Dogwood tree, or get killed if I walked too close to the road, the pond, or the quarry.

"She spies on her like a communist, just looking for reasons to criticize me," Momma complained to Daddy.

Occasionally, Daddy promised to talk it over with Nana. Other times he defended his mother, explaining that she was concerned about me, or that she got a kick out of watching me play. Momma usually said she'd like to give Nana a good kick, but sometimes she just slammed a door and said nothing.

Nana would deal with me herself, or wait on Daddy to come home from work. By then he'd be tired or have a headache and wouldn't want to get Momma started in a tantrum.

With a heavy heart, I ignored Nana and climbed inside the car, where I immediately shoved the key in the ignition and started the engine.

Keeping in mind Nana's repeated prediction that I'd end up at the bottom of the quarry one day, I paused with my hand on the gearshift. It couldn't be that hard to shift into reverse, otherwise, Momma wouldn't pull the car up to the very edge when she was mad at Daddy or Nana, which was almost every day.

Nana yanked the car door opened and pulled me out. I felt another jackrabbit in her heaving chest as she hugged me close and choked out a brand new threat. "Penny Sue, you're going to miss me after you cause me to have a heart attack."

The words were harsh but her tone wasn't. I was sure I could calm her nerves before we passed the Oak tree, and make her forget that I had done anything wrong by the time we reached her house.

"Momma said I could," I cried. "She gave me the keys."

I would regret those words for years, and blame them for destroying the lives of everyone around me, especially my own.

www.ingramcontent.com/pod-product-compliance
Lightning Source LLC
Chambersburg PA
CBHW020407150626
46554CB00012B/403